Inside Outlaw

By

Douglas Eagen

I would like to thank Tom Bird, Ramajon, and Sojourn Publishing.

Your guidance and inspiration has been a key factor along the way.

Most of all I would like to thank my partner in life Dawn.

Your encouragement and belief in me is a gift I never thought I would have.

Introduction

Inside Outlaw is a tale about the ordinary days of a modern day outlaw. Follow Jimmy Star Two Fingers, and his chihuahua Snoop as they travel the deserts of the southwest running drugs from the Mexican border, while looking for a love they lost some time ago.

Jimmy crosses paths with bikers, bandits, aging locals, lovers, new friends, and despicable adversary's in his journeys across life.

Jimmy happens upon Demry, a mining town long past it's prime, during it's yearly town celebration. Looking for a bite to eat Jimmy meets Claudette Burns, a lifelong resident of Demry. Outspoken to say the least, and looking for a friend herself, Jimmy accompanies her to the festivities.

What follows is a glimpse into the everyday hopes, dreams, aspirations, and pitfalls of a not so everyday man. Jimmy's past and present collide when unusual circumstances occur that make him take a close look at himself, his surroundings, and what he really wants out of life.

Between these pages you will find a delightful tale of a New Modern Western, complete with damsels and dastardly deeds. Fortunately for Jimmy though, his unfortunate circumstances may just be the best thing that ever happened to him and lead him to the life he always dreamed of.

I hope you enjoy this tale of the first of my many Lost Sailors, Jimmy Star Two Fingers.

Douglas Eagen

Chapter 1

J immy Star Two Fingers tapped the temperature gauge of his Dodge Astro van in hopes it would recede by itself. But this time, he knew the engine was close to overheating. He twirled the hair of his long grey beard, thinking he could get a few more miles down the road. But if he waited too long, he also knew he ran the risk of blowing the engine. "At least the wipers are still working," he said to himself.

The long black road he took through the Arizona desert was taking a toll on his vehicle and his nerves.

Twenty pounds of high-grade marijuana were stashed in a secret compartment underneath the spare tire. He had room for more, but this is all he took for this trip. All he had to do was to get to Colorado, where he would unload it to his acquaintances and turn a tidy profit.

"Just my luck—rain in Arizona. It never rains in October." He took his sleeve and rubbed the thin film of moisture from the inside of his windshield. It made his shirt smell like antifreeze. That was it. This was as far as he would get tonight.

Through his horn-rimmed glasses, he saw a little pull-off that led to a one-lane dirt road. This would have to work for tonight.

As he turned off the engine, he could hear it hissing, and the radiator was making small pinging noises. He got out under the vehicle to check, but it was useless in this deluge. Everything looked like it was dripping from the undercarriage of the van. All he could hope for was that it was just water from the road, and that it wouldn't be too expensive to fix if he could not do it himself.

This budget trip left him too little to spare until he got to Colorado and turned his freight. He got back into the van and pushed back his soaking hair from his eyes. It was hot, wet, and smelled like antifreeze in the van. "Well, at least, it doesn't smell like pot in here. Not yet at least," he said as he reached for the half joint in his ashtray. Just before lighting it up, his Chihuahua climbed into his lap from the passenger seat.

"Snoop! You're finally up. You slept through all the excitement. How is it that you always know when I am about to get stoned?"

Snoop curled up in the soft spot just above Jimmy's belt line and began licking his paws and underbelly. Jimmy pushed the seat back and put the flame of the lighter to the tip of the joint. He took a couple of long tokes, exhaling slowly, and filled the air with smoke. He cracked the window a bit and watched the smoke escape softly into the night. The red amber from the tip of the joint was all he could see. The clouds had blocked any light from the stars, and he was far from any cities or homes on this humid October night. The sound of rain played its own tune against the roof of the van. The only other noise was of his lips hitting the joint and Snoop licking away at his paws.

As the sensation of being stoned slowly took over, Jimmy lay back and listened to a story that played over and over in his mind for some years now. *Someday, she will return, Jimmy. Someday, you will see her again. But today was not that day.* His eyes slowly closed and he fell asleep. The joint went out by itself and dropped from his hand to the floor.

Chapter 2

J immy awoke to Snoop, whose front paws were on his chest and its tongue licking the side of his face. Jimmy started off not really liking dogs too much, but with his many trips to the border, he and Snoop became good friends, and Snoop turned out to be an excellent traveling companion. Besides, Jimmy had heard somewhere that the drug sniffing dogs had a hard time detecting anything if a dog was in the car.

He cocked his neck back, allowing Snoop to get underneath his chin, and then leaned forward, covering him with his long beard. Stroking the short hairs on Snoop's back before his eyes were opened, he could feel the sun on his face, but he wasn't quite ready to face the day.

As was often the case, when he opened his eyes, he wasn't really sure where he was. He had, through his years, awoken to so many different roads, parking lots, campgrounds, and rest areas that it would usually take the act of opening his eyes to get his bearings on the day and the night before.

Snoop began to moan. "Okay Snoop, I'm up."

Jimmy looked out over the Sonoran desert. He was glad he was here. He opened the door and Snoop jumped down using the running board as a step before his short legs hit the ground.

"Don't go too far, Snoop. Could be snakes out there; might swallow you whole if you're not careful." Snoop sniffed the tire, and then was out of sight around the front of the van.

Jimmy sat up and rubbed his eyes, his gaze still towards the Sonoran Desert. He looked into the rearview mirror. His bright blue eyes smiled back at him. The crow's feet around the corners of his eyes always seemed a little bigger in the morning. The rims and arms of his glasses would cover them up, making them less noticeable as the day went on. "How the hell did you start getting old, Jimmy," he said to himself as he gingerly got out of the van.

Poking his head around the seat and the floor, he found what was left of last night's joint. He put it in his mouth and lit it up. A few short tokes got it burning. Leaning against the side of the van, he took a few more tokes until the ember stung his fingers. He held the side of the van as he limped around the back and opened the door. Splashing some water on his face, he looked at the unmade bed and wondered why he always tended to fall asleep so often on the driver's seat when he had this nice comfortable bed in the back. That's when he remembered her face sleeping in the back with him.

They were together for two years, but that was longer than he had been with any other woman. He pictured her lying there, smoking a cigarette. He didn't particularly like cigarettes. But he didn't mind when Crystal was attached to the other end of one. Her long legs would lean up against the shelves along the sidewall where his books were kept. She would take long drags and blow out smoke rings. She really did not like to talk to him, until she had her first morning smoke immediately upon waking up. But once she did start talking, she rarely stopped.

Brushing these thoughts aside, he called for his dog. "Snoop, where are you, boy?"

Snoop never wandered too far from the van, and he came running and tugged at Jimmy's shoelaces with his small mouth. "There you are, boy. You find any snakes, spiders, scorpions, ticks, coyotes?" Snoop continued to pull at his shoelaces. "Didn't see any cops out there, did ya? No? How about a mechanic?"

Jimmy's mind drifted into the scenery for a moment—the large saguaro cactus dwarfing the low oaks, chollas, barrel cactus, junipers, and dirt and rocks. "No, okay, come on up here." Despite his short legs, Snoop was able to jump into the back of the van. His bowls awaited him, and Jimmy filled one with water and one with food. He looked up at Jimmy before putting his little head into his meal. Jimmy wondered what his little dog saw when he looked up at him like that. Was he just a meal ticket, or was there some deeper understanding in their connection that he just wasn't seeing. "Wow, I am freaking stoned!"

Snoop finished up, and Jimmy put his food away. He wondered what it would have been like if he had gotten a bigger dog. "I'm glad you weren't born a St. Bernard, Snoop. I'd barely afford to feed you." Snoop turned his neck and eagerly accepted Jimmy's fingers scratching and rubbing his face.

Unbuttoning the top of his shirt, Jimmy stuck his nose towards his chest. Inhaling deeply, he decided he didn't smell too bad. "Eh, we'll get one more day out of this."

While peeing in the bushes, Jimmy thought to himself, *Why do I always pee towards a bush even if no one else is around?* He laid the thought down to the strength of the pot. "Man, pot never used to make me think this much." Then another strange thought entered his head. *Man, pot is like brain food!* He could feel his belly jiggle as he chuckled.

Now, he would have to get down to business. He opened up the hood of the van. The reservoir holding the antifreeze was almost empty, and he could see the green liquid forming pools along the bottom of the radiator. "Shit! I hope it is not too bad." He laid out a tarp under the engine. His swollen knee didn't want to bend, and he needed to use the grille and bumper to lower himself underneath. He wiped away the antifreeze and saw it was coming from the seal around the water pump. "Well, at least it's not oil."

But it was a leak nonetheless and beyond what he could, or was willing, to fix on the side of the road. Being a veteran of the road, and especially the back roads, he always carried extra antifreeze, oil, brake fluid, tools, food, and water—all neatly tucked into the nooks and crannies he had built into his road home. In the winters, he would stay down South, and this would be his last run to Colorado before the high mountain winter set in.

He filled the radiator to the top before cranking the engine. He crossed his fingers that he would not hear any loud pops or grinding noises. He turned the key and sighed with relief. The old Astro purred to life like he hoped she would. The van would need to warm up before he could check it for leaks. He grabbed a hairbrush from his console and brushed his wiry hair, wincing when the brush would hit a knot and pull his head to one side. Warmed and ready,

Jimmy leaned beneath the van in hopes of identifying the trouble spots. As far as he could tell, it was leaking from the water pump. Drops of antifreeze were dripping out from the water pump seal. "Not good," he told himself. It could go at any time, and it would probably be sooner than later. "Come on, Snoop, we got to go."

Back on the pavement, he kept a steady eye on the temperature gauge and stopped every twenty minutes to let it cool down and add more fluid.

Jimmy had not taken this route in awhile. He always switched up his routes. He didn't want his vehicle to become to familiar. But also in hopes that someday he would come across Crystal again.

Over time this hope started to fade, but the spark he felt in his heart would not allow him to think he would never see her again.

He wasn't sure if she would even talk to him, but he at least needed to apologize and let her know how deeply ashamed he was of his actions towards her. The last time he saw her, she was slamming the back door of the van. Her pack was slung over one shoulder and her purse over the other. "I love you, Jimmy Star Two Fingers. But this time, you pushed my nerves too far."

"Well, darling, don't let the door hit you in the ass on your way down the road. Adi-fuckin'-os to you, too!

As he pulled away, he looked in the rearview mirror. Crystal had made her way across the road with one arm out, trying to thumb a ride; the other held her middle finger pointing high in the air. Over the road noise, he could hear her screaming. "Fuck you, Jimmy Star Two Fingers!"

Chapter 3

Creeping slowly up the road, Jimmy would pull to the side when another vehicle would speed up to him from behind, letting them pass with ease. The old Astro had treated him well over the years, and he planned on keeping her around for a few more.

He knew of a small town off the main road that he had passed through several times on his journeys, and then he tried to think of what day it was. "Shit! It's Saturday." He knew that the probability of finding a mechanic open today were slim. But he had to try anyway.

He pulled into Demry around 11:00. Despite it being October, the temperature was climbing close to 90. He thanked old Astro for getting him this far. The temperature gauge was past halfway but not pegged into the red.

A banner hung between two poles at the beginning of town. "Welcome to Demry days." It reminded him of an old song he couldn't remember, and he began to whistle it. That caught Snoop's attention, and he bounded into his lap and began tugging at his beard with his small teeth.

"You like that song, Snoop? Good, you get to sing the next verse! I wonder what Demry days are, Snoop?" He knew it was way past rodeo season, but he bet there was some kind of food.

Jimmy pulled up the main street. Cars and trucks lined both sides, and the side streets looked full also. Lots of people were walking, mostly all in the same direction. Demry's charm was only outdone by its decrepitude. It looked like a picture out of the fifties, probably when the mines were in their heyday, and when people were making money hands over fist.

Concrete buildings with large display windows lined both sides of the road. Awnings gave shade to the passersby. Jimmy did a double take as he passed one store that had a Woolworths sign. A woman with long brown hair came out with two kids in tow. "Holy shit, Snoop, there's a Woolworths still open. Remember that one in Santa Fe? They had the best Frito pie!"

He could see that the road was closed a few blocks ahead, and he turned down a side street. A few blocks down, he found a place to park in an older neighborhood full of brick houses. The dirt yards were mostly bare, except for low shrubs and cactus.

"Good, a place as any for now, Snoop. Looks like there is a celebration going on. I don't think we will find a mechanic, but I bet we will find some fry bread!"

Jimmy sat for a moment and took a few deep breaths. "Okay, the temperature gauge is going down. The pot is all stashed." He looked into the mirror. His face seemed presentable enough. He tied his beard up with hair ties: one at the bottom; one at the top. He put on his shades and gave one last look into the mirror. "If not for the collar of this Hawaiian shirt, I'd say I look like a badass biker."

He was sure he would see a few bikers out today, when many would be out for their weekend scoot. Jimmy knew that bikers and long hairs, despite their sometimes differing views, would usually give a nod to each other along the road. Both were a breed apart from each other, but more alike than from the regular working folk. Jimmy had worked with bikers over the years. The bikers had the money, balls, and connections to get the goods over the border, but rarely would they take it much further. That's where guys like Jimmy came in. He had learned a lot about bikers over the years. Mostly, if you're straight up with them, you will be all right. He made it a point not to go out drinking with them and not to get too chummy with them. That just made them nervous. And there is nothing scarier than a nervous biker, except maybe a nervous cop.

Jimmy took note of his clothes. His shirt was fairly clean and, despite falling asleep in it, was not too wrinkled. His jeans were faded but clean. He thought that on a day like today, he should really be wearing shorts, but with his knee all swollen the way it was, he didn't want to bring too much attention to himself. He would bring his cane with him, in case his knee bothered him too much. The hard hickory shaft was dark and straight with a silver eagle handle at the top. He put a leash on Snoop and got out of the van.

Chapter 4

W hen Jimmy got out of his van, a woman he figured to be in her seventies was coming out of the house he had parked in front of. She was wearing a blue pastel pantsuit and thick white sneakers. Her face was bright with lipstick and blush. Her stiff hair was pulled back in a scarf sticking up a few inches above her head.

As she closed her gate, Jimmy asked, "Hey, is it all right if I park here?"

"Of course it is, young man. My property ends right here at the gate."

"It's been a long time since I have been called a young man."

She stood back, looked him up and down with her hand on her hip, and said, "Son, you're still a young man."

"Well, thank you kindly, ma'am."

"You might be young but you don't need to be *ma'aming* me. I'm not as old as I may seem to be."

"Sorry for the indiscretion, uh, Miss—?

She quickly cut him off. "And don't you be *missin'* me neither! My husband has been gone for some time now, but I still consider myself a missus, Mrs. Claudette Burns."

She looked up at him and asked, "And you are?"

"Uh, Jimmy."

"And?" she asked.

Jimmy shrugged, "And what?"

"You got a last name, Jimmy, or is it Jimmy And What?" Claudette smiled and brushed some lint off her shoulder.

"Uh, yeah, I do. It's Jimmy Star Two Fingers." Jimmy gave her a slight bow. "At your service."

"Excuse me, did you say it was Jimmy Star Two Fingers? That sounds Native American to me. You don't look Native American. Mixed blood?"

"No, actually, I'm Irish."

"Irish!" she exclaimed. "Now how in tarnation does an Irishman get a name like that?"

"Long story, "Jimmy rolled his eyes and chuckled.

"I bet it is, Mr. Two Fingers. I bet it is."

"Please call me Jimmy."

Looking down, she asked, "And who is this little cutie pie here?"

"Oh, this is Snoop, my partner in crime."

Claudette crossed her arms. "Now, you I am not so sure about, but this little one doesn't look like any criminal I have ever seen." Claudette slowly bent over and scratched Snoop on the head.

"Don't let him fool you; he is a real killer!

"I bet he is, Mr. Two Fingers."

"So, what is this Demry days about, Mrs. Burns?"

"Oh, please, Claudette will do just fine. Not from here then, I take it?"

"No, just passing through."

"Well, lucky you, then. Demry days are about the best time to be here. This weekend and the rodeo, but that was back in July. You missed the dance last night, but the fair is going on all day today, and tomorrow is the annual town picnic."

"Right on then. I guess I'll be heading that way."

"In that case, if you don't mind being seen with an older woman, walk with me. I'll show you around a bit.

"Not at all. As long as you don't mind being seen with a couple of outlaws in your own town, it would be an honor."

"Not at all, Mr. Two Fingers. Scofflaws have always been some of my favorite people. Not too many of them left around here, though."

"Where'd they all go? This place seems pretty tame to me."

"Oh, Mr. Two Fingers, let me tell you. Back in the days, right after the war, this place was just a bustling with miners and game halls. Seems money was just a flying into people's hands, and the—well, how do I say?—unsavory types were all here to make sure it was flying right back out. I tell you, this place reached a fever back then that was just too hard to ignore and not take a little part in."

"And you're trying to tell me that a sweet woman like yourself took part in these..." Jimmy cleared his throat. "...unsavory activities."

"Took part, indeed, Mr. Two Fingers. Didn't take much to get me out of the house those days. You see, my husband worked the twelve-to-eight shift at the mine. He'd come home and get cleaned up and take me out dancing a couple of nights a week. Oh, how I loved to dance...." Claudette stopped walking and paused into some faraway dance floor in the past. "Some saw that in itself as being unsavory, but there was a lot more than that going on here in Demry, a whole lot more, I tell you. But those days are behind us."

They began walking down the cracked sidewalk, Claudette holding onto Jimmy's elbow.

"So where are you coming from, Mr. Two Fingers?"

"Please call me Jimmy."

"Okay, then, what brings you to Demry on this fine day?"

"Well, Claudette, I've been on the road, just checking out the sights, you know. And last night, I started having car trouble, and I need a mechanic. Demry was the closest town around."

Jimmy wondered why he and many others always referred to it simply as "car trouble" in a conversation. Perhaps it was an easier way to not impose impending doom should it be worse than expected.

"Nothing too serious, I hope."

"No, none too serious but more than my tool kit can handle on the side of the road. So I pulled into town looking for a mechanic and realized it was Saturday and am probably out of luck. Saw the banners and decided to look for some county fair food."

"I'm afraid you're right about the mechanics. Gus Meyers always takes the weekends off; he used to stay open on Saturdays. But ever since his son set out for California, he says it's too much for him."

A flash of the ocean passed before Jimmy's eyes. He had searched the coast around San Diego for some time for Crystal, but every time he saw long blonde hair, his heart would jump. And there was too much blonde hair to go around or sift through.

"Then there is Billy Simpson's garage, but his wife just passed, and they are holding services on Monday. He might not be open for a few days. He took it real hard when they found out she was sick."

Claudette's slow pace of walking was just fine with Jimmy. His knee had been feeling better, but after a few days in a row of driving, it "gets all stiffed up," to use his own words. The cane was just a precaution in case he stayed on it for too long. Jimmy knew that some of his short walks had turned into the next morning. Not all of it walking. A friendly tavern or a card game has been known to lead him astray. Then there are the libraries that have always captured his fascination since he was a kid.

With Snoop in tow and Claudette in one arm, they made their way down Mesquite Street towards the park. The few cars that passed them slowed at the sight of Claudette arm in arm with a strange and much younger long-haired man.

Jimmy didn't give it much attention, but wondered at the effort and fascination others put into their neighbors' business. He knew that with some folks, it was genuine concern, especially when that concern was directed towards the elders. But deep down, he felt it was the latest bit of juicy gossip that kept most towns alive.

Claudette also noticed the slowing vehicles, the sideward glances, and the semi-shocked faces.

"Don't you pay them no mind, Jimmy," Claudette said with a wave of her hand, as a brown sedan sped back up after slowing down to have a look. "People around here just can't mind their own beeswax."

"No problem here, Claudette. Besides, if someone decides to get cross over you and me, I'll just sick old Snoop on them. Ain't that right, Snoop!"

At the sound of his own name, Snoop doubled back between his leash, taking a moment to lift his head from the endless amount of scents he tracked along the ground.

"You know why most people come by your house to pay condolences when a loved one passes, Jimmy?"

"I suppose it is out of respect."

"Nope, that's not it at all, not for most of them. Now, there are all your close friends, families, and those that you work with. But them others, the ones that have never been to your house the whole time you are alive, they show up when you're dead...."

"I'm not following you, Claudette."

Jimmy felt her squeeze a little closer, and she looked at him as she spoke.

"Nope, them ones that never set a foot in your house. They finally get a chance to snoop around."

Unnoticed to Claudette, Snoop again doubled back at the sound of the name he knew so well.

"Yes, indeed, they come bringing casseroles and offering to help with your chores and such. But, mostly, they want to see the inside of your house, see what kind of plates you use, check out how worn your furniture is. Mostly, they like to see how your bathroom looks. You can learn a lot about someone by taking a little peek around their bathroom."

Jimmy shook his head and pulled on Snoop's leash to get him to move from his latest point of interest.

"And the men, you notice them after niceties heading straight to the garage. See what's in there to divvy up!" Claudette ended her little rant with a huff and picked up her pace a little bit. Jimmy noticed she was breathing a little heavier, and sweat was forming on her brow just beneath the bangs of her stiff hair. Another car slowed down, and the driver crooked his neck as he passed. Claudette wagged her finger at the driver. "Mind your own business, you two-timing old fool!"

Jimmy laughed. "Seems like you've been paying a close mind on your neighbors as well, Claudette."

She slowed her pace. "I guess maybe you're right, Jimmy. Oooh, these nosy old farts just make me so damn mad!"

"Must be some young people around here somewhere," Jimmy said while looking at the ages of the cars, the curtains in the windows, the choice of lawn furniture, and the lack of toys in the yards. Those led him to believe this was literally a dying town.

"Oh, there are some young people around, more than you might think. You'll see them in the park today with their kids. People that love Demry really love it. And those that don't, well, they skedaddle as soon as they can."

Chapter 5

The heat of the day began to congregate in its usual places—collars, armpits, and brows all took their turn with a shake, wipe, or scratch. Jimmy was no stranger to this congregation, spending most of his time in warm climates. Although his beard was tied, the growth under his chin that had been left unchecked by a razor became uncomfortable in the hot desert sun.

Upon entering the Demry town park, Jimmy noticed collars being unbuttoned and bandanas and handkerchiefs being at the ready. A few parasols donned the elbows of a few of the more experienced woman used to the days of early autumn heat.

Walking into the park was like walking back into his childhood, albeit far from whatever he had once considered one of his many homes, mostly in New Jersey around Fort Dix.

It wasn't until a few children from the Paint Your Face booth came running up and asked, "Mister, can we please pet your dog?" that he realized he was getting closer to Claudette's age than their own.

"Well, sure you can, kids. He especially likes it when you scratch behind the ears."

The girl with stars painted on her forehead and whose blonde hair was tied back in pigtails got down on her hands and knees, right at eye level with Snoop.

"Hello, little doggie, what's your name?"

Jimmy felt so big standing next to them; his tall figure towered above the small children. "His name is Snoop."

The three girls giggled at this. The little red-headed girl, with glasses that were clearly too big for her face and with rainbows painted on her cheeks, said, "Snoop, that's funny. I like that name."

"He likes it, too," Jimmy said.

The girl on the ground playing with Snoop looked up. "How do you know he likes it?"

Jimmy grinned. "He told me so. Curled right up to my ear one day and said"—Jimmy changed the pitch of his voice and tried to make it higher—"'Thanks for naming me Snoop. I really like that name.'"

The three girls were quiet for a moment. Then the little star-faced girl on the ground broke the silence.

"Nuh-uh, dogs don't talk like that." And she went back to rubbing him on his stomach.

"Looks like he likes you, little one."

"I like him, too."

After a few moments, Claudette told the girls to get a move on; their mamas were probably looking for them.

As they walked away, Jimmy told Claudette, "I think he was starting to like that."

"They were, too. Before you know it, they would all want to take a turn on the ground with him, and I for one am getting mighty hungry. Let's get over to the food booths before it gets too hot to eat."

The tourists didn't seem to notice the unusual couple arm in arm, but as they walked towards the middle of the park by the pavilion, heads began to turn. Jimmy noticed it this time and felt like the stranger he was in this town. But he was not deterred by their stares or the whispers under their breath. Jimmy hadn't cared about what most people thought for a long time now, and he knew that he had seen, and been, through more than these folks could ever want to deal with. He was a man alone in this world. If a strange woman wanted to be on his arm for a little while for a stroll through the park, they could all go to hell. And if they wanted to start something with them, he would help them in getting there.

They made a slight bend around the pavilion to where the food courts were set up. The Daughters of the Revolution were set up with a bake sale. As they were walking by it, the whispers behind cupped hands began in earnest. Seeing this, Claudette scooched a little bit closer to Jimmy and led him towards the booth. "Come on, Jimmy, we are going to put an end to this right now, or at least have a little fun." She looked up at him and asked, "You in for a little fun?"

"What do you have in mind, honey?"

"You'll see!"

"Never a dull moment with you around, I bet. I'm in!"

They turned and marched quickly up to the booth, cutting in front of the two women who were part of the gossip. The women behind the booth were clearly embarrassed as Claudette put Jimmy's hand in hers and looked the women right in the eye. "Hello, Deidra," and then with a nod towards the other, she just said, "Sally."

Both returned the gesture with a nod and said, "Good afternoon, Claudette."

Jimmy stood and stared at the women with a big smile on his face, as he had no idea what Claudette had in mind. But, as far as he was concerned, he saw no harm in having a little fun. Sally looked up from his beard and into his eyes. Jimmy winked. It was clear to him that if she could have run right out of there, she would have.

Claudette asked Deidra what the best things on the table were.

"I guess it's got to be Doris McMillan's crumb cake or Annie Parko's potica. Either way, you can't go wrong."

"I'll have a piece of the crumb cake, and Jimmy, dear, what would you care for?"

Taking his cue, Jimmy pulled on his beard and twisted it between his fingers. "Well, sugar plumb, since I am all out of money, I'd sure love it if I could get a piece of that potica bread." By the looks on their faces they were clearly shocked by Jimmy's comment. "Oh, and girls, make sure it is a nice big piece! I sure did work up an appetite today." He pulled Claudette closer and put his arm around her shoulder.

They quickly served them up their order. "No charge today for you, Claudette, seeing you have a guest in town."

Jimmy was taking a bite when Claudette said, "Oh, he is no guest, ladies. He is my hired lover." Jimmy coughed and spit some of the bread out on the ground.

She took his arm and led him away from the booth. He took one last look back, and Deidra and Sally were both standing there with their mouths wide open. They were a few yards away when Claudette stopped and turned to them.

"A girl's got to get some loving somehow." She gave them a thumbs-up and walked away.

When Jimmy finally stopped laughing, he said, "Mrs. Burns, I do believe you turned their ears red. What was that all about?"

"Too many damn nosy people around here, especially those two. They spread gossip like you wouldn't believe. Half the town believes them and half don't. Years back, they had me sleeping with my husband's boss at the mine, just so he could keep his job."

"Were you?" Jimmy asked.

"Oh, hell no!" and she playfully slapped him in his ribs with the back of her hand. "But now, you big fella, that might be different."

"You couldn't afford me, remember? I'm a pro."

Claudette laughed. "Oh, dear, I hope I didn't embarrass you too much back there."

They kept walking until they reached the stage where the high school band was playing a patriotic tune. A small bald man in baggy pants and a collar shirt and tie was conducting them. His jacket had seen better days as it clung tightly to him.

Jimmy put his finger in his ear and poked around. "Wow! These kids need some practice."

"Yes, they do, Jimmy." Claudette took her arm from him. "You don't mind me calling you Mr. Two Fingers? It just sounds so much more—I don't know—glamorous than Jimmy."

"Call me what you'd like."

"Well Mr. Two Fingers, there have been so many cutbacks at the school that these kids barely get a chance to play. You see that man conducting? There is not even really a music teacher. He is Mr. Cantino, and he is the janitor. When the board said they were going to do away with the music program, old Ben there stepped up and did what he could."

"There have been so many cut backs at the school. Kids and families have been leaving left and right. Damn shame what's happening to this town."

"Why is everybody leaving?"

"Price of copper mostly. When it's down as far as it has been, the mine cuts back. Price goes up, the mine gets busy. The price goes down and...well, you drove through. You see what it's like. Good people losing good paying jobs, though. Hard enough to support your own kids, nonetheless a whole school and all its programs. Anyway, you are right. Those kids were hurting my ears.

Chapter 6

The heat of the day was upon them as they made their way down the artist aisle. Banners and signs advertising quilts, candles, homemade jams, silver jewelry, paintings, and dream catchers. There was even a booth placed far from the rest due to the noise that was turning out baseball bats on a lathe. This was by far the most popular booth. Young boys and their fathers lined up, waiting their turn. Mr. Jennings, the man with the booth, could turn out a bat in twenty minutes. And with a soldering iron, he would engrave your name on it. It was a Demry tradition to have a Jennings bat, as they were known. Every boy in Demry would get their own bat at one time or another. Mr. Jennings made sure of this.

"Seems the boys got the best part of the park," Jimmy said.

"Ol' Mr. Jennings always does have the most popular booth."

The bandanas and kerchiefs were out in full force, and the parasols that occupied elbows earlier were now in full bloom twirling in hands fortunate enough to bring them.

The only ones who didn't seem bothered by the heat were the children.

"How long do these Demry days go on, Claudette?"

Claudette had let go of Jimmy's arm somewhere between the bandstand and the handmade pottery booth. She had caused enough ruckuses for one day to keep all the gossipers at their wit's end for weeks.

"Well, Jimmy, like I think I said earlier, you missed the dance last night. Today is the fair. Tonight will be an outdoor concert and fireworks. And tomorrow, well, tomorrow is the day that nobody misses. The town picnic is about the best day of the weekend. Then that's it. Place about folds up after that...until Christmas. Get some traffic on the weekends from Phoenix, but that's about all." Claudette stopped and sat on one of the benches. Both of her hands were busy rubbing her lower back, and then her thighs. "I've got to keep the blood flowing. Whew! I tire easy these days, Mr. Two Fingers. This old body sure ain't what it used to be. Used to dance every night. But, boy, last night sure did tucker me out. But you go on ahead now, if you want. I'll be fine here."

"No, not at all. I'll sit with you a spell." Jimmy used his cane to lower himself down to the bench seat. His beard hid the grimace that had crossed his lips due to the pain and stiffness in his knee.

"So what's kept you here all these years, Claudette?"

She put her elbows on the bench top and looked towards the pavilion. "That's a good question, Mr. Two Fingers. I was born here and guess I never knew I could leave if I wanted to. My roots are here, my family is here, and it really is all I've ever known. I was raised by the mine, married my husband here. All my friends are here, at least those that are left alive. I still have plenty of family here, mostly cousins now—them and their children. We get together on Sundays after church most weeks." Claudette swatted at a fly buzzing around her head and neck. "Get away from me. But not tomorrow, though. We will all be down here for the town picnic, so I guess that's still getting together."

Suddenly, Claudette raised her nose to the air. "Mmmmm...mmmm...mmmm. You smell that, Mr. Two Fingers?"

Jimmy put his nose up and took a big whiff. "I smell something good."

"If I'm not mistaken, that is Jenny Ostara's fry bread and chili. She comes down from the reservation every year for Demry days. Almost as much of a tradition for those boys getting ball bats is getting lined up for her fry bread and chili before she sells out." Claudette put her hands down and lifted herself slowly off the bench. "My favorite part of Demry days, Jenny's fry bread. Come on, let's go get some before that line gets too long."

The line was long, but they finally got to the front. Jenny Ostara was a small round woman who appeared to be in her fifties from the Gila Indian reservation. Her long black hair was tied back in a bandana. Her hands moved quickly as the line went through. She knew most of the people, greeting them by name, as they walked through the park. When Claudette and Jimmy got to the front, Jenny got a big smile on her face. "Claudette, how are you today? I'm so glad you made it to see me!"

"Oh, Jenny, you know I wouldn't miss you today. It's my main reason for coming."

"Oh, stop now. You have plenty of reasons for coming."

"Two today?" Jenny asked.

Claudette turned to Jimmy and patted him on the elbow. "Oh, yes, two today, dear."

Jenny's hands kept moving, and, with a nod of her head towards Jimmy, she asked, "New boyfriend, Claudette."

Claudette smiled and put her head close to Jenny's ear. "That's what I'm telling everybody today." Then she put her hand in a small fist and shook her arm. "Getting them all riled up."

"Good for you. Some of these people need a good riling up walking around here like they half dead or something."

"Well, most of them are." They both laughed as Jenny handed them their food.

"How are all of your grandchildren doing?" Claudette asked.

"Oh, boy, I can hardly keep up. I have eleven now," Jenny said while shaking her head.

"Eleven? Oh, lucky you, Jenny."

"I know. I am blessed. A few of them running around here today. Come back later and you can meet them."

"Oh, I sure would like that."

"Bye-bye now."

As they walked back to the benches, Jimmy wondered what it would be like to have that many grandchildren. The work it must take seemed insurmountable to him. But what he wouldn't give to have a large family to love and adore. In fact, there wasn't much he wouldn't give to have any family at all. His mother passed when he was a child. And his father, whom he barely spoke with since being discharged from the service when he was a teen, also passed some years back. A small hollow place in his heart sat empty, dreaming of what it would be like to have a child or two to call his own.

Eating the fry bread and chili helped to hide the hole as he let the flavors run through his mouth and slide down past his tongue to his waiting belly. "Oh my god! This is the best fry bread I've ever had, Claudette!"

Jimmy hunched over his food in hopes of keeping it off his shirt and out of his beard.

"Jenny does make the best."

They both went on eating; all the while, Jimmy was giving Snoop small bits under the table. The picnic table they sat at was flanked by many other tables until they made long rows. There were several rows, and people at first sat away from each other, but now the spaces were beginning to fill in. A few clouds began to form, and shadows quickly moved up and down the tables as they passed in front of the sun. A blues band began to play from the bandstand, and even from a distance, Jimmy could tell they had considerably more talent than the band before them.

Claudette sat across from Jimmy, and even though they were apart, the local crowd still looked over their shoulders as they walked by. She seemed to not notice, but Jimmy caught her eyes several times locked in a glance with a neighbor or two. It didn't seem to bother her to stare someone down, but Jimmy felt bad for having caused her this grief in her own town. Nonetheless, he enjoyed the company of sharing conversation and a meal with another human being. The road had been his life for many years, and, other than a few interludes of staying put, it was hard to get any sort of social life going.

"So, you told me your car was breaking down, but why are you really here, Mr. Two Fingers? Demry is a long way off from the regular tourist crowd."

"Well, to be perfectly honest with you, I am looking for a girl."

Claudette batted her eyes and put one hand up against the side of her head in a pose. "Well, honey, look no further! My husband has been gone for twelve years now. I think it's time I jump back in."

Jimmy laughed and wiped his mouth with his napkin. "Oh, now, Claudette, I'm not sure I could handle a woman as sassy as yourself!"

She put her arm down and leaned her chin on her hands. "Oh, honey, believe you me, I'm not that sassy anymore. I just talk a good show."

Jimmy watched the crowd as it got larger and louder. The boys in the corner began swinging their bats, trying to outdo each other by hitting imaginary home runs. The food lines began to get longer, and the smoke from the vendors cooking were making small low clouds around the booths. A small breeze began to kick up loose napkins and paper plates, sending their owners scurrying after them in an attempt to keep the park clean.

As he stared into the distance, Claudette could tell that loneliness clung to him like a cloak. He had a nice smile underneath all of that hair, but it was his eyes that told her the truth. It was almost as if they broke down watching as the families pass by. She let a few moments of silence pass and then put her hand on top of his.

"So, I am taking it this is one girl in particular you are looking for, Mr. Two Fingers."

"How'd you guess?"

"Mr. Two Fingers, beneath that bravado you're toting, you got a look of a forlorn man who is far away from home.

Mmm...hmmm, otherwise known as lovesick. By the way, where do you call home, Mr. Two Fingers?"

"You know that van I pulled up in? That's home." Snoop jumped up into his lap, and he began scratching behind his ears. "Isn't it, boy?"

"No home. Well, that ain't right. Where are your kin."

"None left to speak of. I was an only child, and my folks are passed. I grew up an army brat, and we never stuck around one place for me to make many friends." Then he looked down and to the side. "None that lasted at least."

"You never married or had any children then either?

"Nope, never could see myself settling down."

Claudette folded her hands together and smiled at him. "Well, now you've got me. I'll be your friend. Well, at least for as long as you're in Demry. Anybody that can put up with me and my shenanigans is worthy of friendship in my book."

"I appreciate your kind words, Claudette, but I probably won't be around very long."

A group of bikers in leather vests and patches were walking in the aisle over from them. Jimmy recognized the one in front. Ringo James and he had met years ago and did business together from time to time. Last time he saw Ringo, Jimmy had a gun pointed at his head.

Ringo was a frighteningly big man. He was 6'10" and 275 lbs. His face was covered in a big bushy beard that was starting to grey around the edges. His bald head set upon shoulders wide and strong enough to plow a field by himself. He caught Jimmy's eye, and they nodded to each other.

They ran into each other from time to time, mostly when doing a deal. His posse today included five other guys of varying heights, weights, and hair lengths, all wearing leather jackets with the same patches.

Claudette had turned her head and watched the bikers pass. When they were out of hearing distance, she told Jimmy, "Demry days brings in all the weirdos, Mr. Two Fingers. Vagrants, bikers, hippies." She put her hand to her mouth and blushed. "Excuse me, present company excluded."

Jimmy sat back and smiled at her with his hands behind his head. His biceps flexed, and Claudette noted that they were quite large and toned. When the sleeves hiked up towards his shoulders, she saw several tattoos but could not make out what they were.

"Now, now, Claudette"—Jimmy smiled—"do I look like a biker or a vagrant to you?"

She leaned over the table and cupped her hands and said, "Hippie."

Jimmy leaned halfway across the table to meet her. Twisting his beard in his hand, he spoke softly to her, "Oh, well. Now, Claudette, you've got yourself confused there, honey. I may have long hair, but I am far from being a hippie. Being a hippie has got its own set of rules that I can't quite abide by.

"Oh Mr. Two Fingers, I do apologize."

"That's quite all right, Claudette. Apology accepted."

"So, Mr. Two Fingers, if you don't mind me asking, who is this particular woman you are fawning over? And what happened?"

Jimmy looked away from her and put Snoop back on the ground. "Oh, Claudette, it was some years back. I met a woman out on the road. We were together for a while, and then she left."

The silence between them allowed the shrill of the crowd to rush in. The silence sat between them until Claudette finally spoke up. "And?"

Jimmy looked up at her. Her mascara was starting to smudge from her wiping the sweat near her eyes.

"And what?" Jimmy said.

"And what? Come now, Mr. Two Fingers. There's got to be more to it than that if you're still feeling this strongly after all this time. Maybe it's none of my business, but it looks like you have more you want to say about it."

Jimmy folded his hands together and put them on the table. "Oh, hell, you got a valid point there, Claudette. It's just that I...I...I never got to say good-bye to her, and it breaks my heart to this day."

"Now, I know this is none of my business, but why'd she leave you, Jimmy?"

Jimmy stared down at the cracks in the wood of the picnic table, tracing one particular one with his eyes all the way to the end of the table. He looked up and saw a man at the end with his collared shirt buttoned to the top. He was berating his wife about something. At first, he was trying to speak under his breath, but he was much too loud to not be heard by those around him.

"You do it because I told you to do it; that's why. Damn it, end of subject!"

The man's tone reminded Jimmy a bit of how his father would speak to him when he was a child. But as a child, he was much less obedient than the woman sitting across from the man with the tight collar.

"Yes, Michael, I'm sorry. I should have listened to you. Please stop," the woman said through her tears.

Jimmy's heart broke as much as hers as he watched her sitting there with her life being slowly taken out of her. He felt like getting up and going over and knocking the man out. But so far, it was none of his business, and he thought better of drawing any more attention to himself.

"So, I am waiting," Claudette said.

"Oh, sorry," Jimmy said, returning his attention to Claudette. "It's just that I can't stand jackasses like that."

"You think he's bad? You should have seen his father. Made him look like a tiddlywink. He'd grab his wife so hard right in front of everybody you could see the bruises before they even got to the car. Spiteful man he was. No one was too sorry to see him go to the other side of the ground, except for maybe his son over there. But I'm sorry, go on."

"Well, she said I was beginning to be mean to her and not being kindly towards her needs."

"That sounds about right in line with most men, Mr. Two Fingers. At least the understanding part. Why were you mean to her? Didn't you love her?"

Jimmy dragged his fingers through his hair and took a deep breath. "To be honest with you, she is the only woman I ever loved. But she was a difficult woman. Always wanting to do things that got in the way of what we were supposed to be doing."

Claudette slapped her hand lightly on the table. "See, that's the problem right there, Jimmy. Men are always thinking they are right in what they are supposed to be doing." Then she cocked her head towards the end of the table. "Like that fool down there."

"And?" Jimmy asked this time.

"And what?" Claudette returned.

Claudette shook a finger at him and pursed her small lips together in the form of a kiss. It made her face look like a fish with her narrow cheeks and high sloping forehead. Then she scrunched her eyes. Jimmy could see her true age come out from underneath the heavy amount of makeup she had on. She took a deep breath and sighed.

"And women don't—well, most women, including myself—don't seem to know why men are always fussing about what we are supposed to be doing all the time. Life is much too short to be fussing over things, unless it has to do with the welfare of your children. Most men just need to relax a bit."

The man in the collared shirt was getting louder, and the people around him were falling silent and moving away from them. He began to scream at his wife. "What did you say to me!?"

She was trying to keep her tears to herself, but Jimmy could tell she was crying. He could tell she used to be pretty before the radiance of her life had been stolen by her husband. Between her muffled cries, he could hear her saying, "Please, Michael, stop. Please, not here, not today. We don't need to do this."

Michael stood up, put his knuckles on the table, and leaned over, so his face was close to hers. She turned her head, not wanting to face him.

He yelled very sternly in her ear, "Don't you ever tell me what to do!"

"Please, Michael, stop it!" She was becoming hysterical, and a crowd started to gather.

Michael stood straight up and said, "Get up! We are leaving!" He took out a handkerchief out of his pocket, wiped the perspiration from his forehead, and then threw it down on the table. The veins in his neck and forehead were sticking out, and his face had gone to a very dark red. "I said we are going now!"

Jimmy could take no more of the woman's suffering. He stood up and winced at the pain in his knee. Snoop scurried beneath his feet. "Hey, pal!" he yelled at Michael. "Why don't you knock it off? Ain't no way to treat a woman, making her cry in public like that."

The woman was shocked and immediately looked towards Jimmy. He could see a little bit of her beauty trying to creep back in behind her swollen eyes.

Michael slowly turned his head towards Jimmy. He was grimacing, and his nostrils were flaring. "What did you say to me!?"

"Seems like that's your best line, buddy," Jimmy answered back.

Those who had gathered fell from their silence and began to chuckle. This infuriated Michael, and he turned his whole body to face Jimmy.

When Jimmy got a good look at how big he was, he said, "Oh shit," under his breath.

"Who the hell do you think you are butting into my business?"

Despite Michael's size, Jimmy found his courage and spoke up. "You are yelling so loud, making it everybody's business. Why you got to make the poor girl cry like that?"

Michael crooked his neck, and Jimmy could swear he heard it crack like in the old gangster movies. It unnerved Jimmy, and he began to come closer to him.

"I suggest you get the hell out of here before I crush your skull, you fucking hippy!"

Jimmy found the timing ironic but took offense to it. He yelled back, "Fuck you asshole!" thinking to himself, *That's a pretty standard answer to kick off a good fight.*

The crowd grew and began to circle the two men.

"Oh, boy," Jimmy said to himself, "great way not to draw attention to yourself." He grabbed his cane, trying to even the odds a little bit, and motioned Michael towards him with his hand.

An elderly man tried to stand between them. With his soft voice and frail body, he looked up at Michael. "Michael, please, don't do this, for Christ's sake. It's Demry days! Your father would not be proud of you."

Jimmy had never seen a man's face turn so red. "Mr. Allen, you're lucky my old man is not around to kick your ass like the way I'm gonna kick this poor sucker's ass any minute now if he doesn't shut the fuck up."

Jimmy knew it was all or nothing now. Hopefully, he could make him mad enough to make a mistake. He was no stranger to fighting, and he knew it could go either way when pure rage was involved. But he even surprised himself when he said, "So, you don't just pick on women, you pick on old men, too. What a piece of shit."

Michael rushed towards Jimmy, throwing Mr. Allen to the side. Just as he was within striking distance, a bald head and leather vest came flashing in front of Jimmy, tackling Michael quickly to the ground.

It was Ringo. He quickly got on top of him and gave him one solid punch to the jaw. Michael's head snapped back, and he quickly covered up.

The crowd was as surprised as Jimmy was. Their reaction was mixed, but he could pick Claudette out above the ruckus, laughing and coughing.

Ringo stood up, staring down at Michael. "That's right. You better lay there. Messing with your woman is one thing. Pushing around an old man is another. You should be ashamed of yourself, you fucking loser!"

Ringo made the motion of trying to kick him, and Michael tried to scramble out of the way. Ringo held back, he knew he had hurt him, no sense in taking it further and risking a night behind bars. He pointed his big hand at Michael, his rings flashing in the sun. "If I see you again today, I'm gonna finish you!"

Jimmy looked around at the crowd. He could see Michael's wife running away and Claudette at the table laughing so hard she was slapping her leg!

Ringo was wiping the dirt and the grass off his hands on the knees of his blue jeans. His gang was laughing and slapping him on the back.

Snoop, who had gotten loose, was running around Michael, who was still on his side lying on the ground, holding his jaw. Blindly, he swatted at Snoop. But Snoop was quick, and he flinched back and bit Michael squarely on the thumb. The crowd began too chuckle.

Jimmy yelled for Snoop. "Get over here, boy! No need to be getting all David and Goliath around here. He learned his lesson."

Michael got up and looked at Ringo. His eyes were seething with anger. He tried to say something, but his jaw was too swollen to work. Ringo looked back, easily towering over him by a half a foot. In his deep husky voice, he told

Michael, "You're lucky I am in a good mood today." Then he put his arm on Michael's back and whispered towards his ear, "Listen to me and listen good. I've got eyes and ears all over this state. If I find out you take your anger and touch your wife"—he pointed to Jimmy—"or come back after this man over here, I'll make sure your arms and jaw never work again. Understand!" He then pulled Michael by the back of the hair, pointed his face towards his, and slowly said, "Now leave."

Michael walked away quickly, looking back several times while holding his jaw. The crowd began to cheer, and Ringo held up both of his giant arms and then let them fall to his sides. He bent his large frame over and picked up Jimmy's cane and handed it to him.

"Here's your cane, sir." And he gave Jimmy a quick wink and a smile.

Jimmy looked at the cane in his hands and then back to Ringo. "Thanks."

"No problem, mister. I hate punks like that—no respect for others. Drives me freaking crazy!" He shook his shoulders and back.

While Ringo was walking away, he turned back to Jimmy and said, "Nice dog!"

His gang was laughing, and Ringo looked at the people still lingering and said, "Show's over, folks. He won't be bothering you again."

Then came a small smattering of applause, as well as the town's number one export, gossip.

Jimmy sat back down across from Claudette. "Well, look at you!" He laughed at the sight of her. Snoop took up position in his lap again, and he scratched his ears. Claudette had laughed so hard she began to cry, and the heavy mascara she was wearing melted, leaving big black streaks running down her cheeks.

"You look like Alice Cooper!" Jimmy said.

"Who?"

"Never mind, but you should take a good look at yourself."

"Oh, Mr. Two Fingers, that certainly was exciting. You sure do know how to start a good party." Claudette's big blue eyes were beaming.

"Well, you know what they say."

Claudette propped her chin on the back of her hands and looked at Jimmy like he was the only man in a town waiting for an answer that never came. She batted her eyes like a cougar in heat, and one of her fake eyelashes fell off and was hanging from the side of her eyelid. Jimmy looked at this poor woman's face and thought it can't get much better, or worse, than this.

"Now, how the hell did that happen?" She pulled a small compact from her purse and took a look at herself. "Oh my! Oh my! Well, I am certainly not going to attract any men like this now, am I?"

"I don't know, Claudette. Is the circus due anytime soon?"

"Oh, stop that, Mr. Two Fingers."

Claudette peeled off her other lash. She then licked a small napkin and began to wipe her face. That just made it worse.

"Oh, Mr. Two Fingers, I'm afraid I can't be walking around like this."

"Sure you can, Claudette. Didn't you just tell me a minute ago that Demry days attracts all the freaks? What'd you say? Uh, bikers, uh, vagrants, hippies." He pointed his finger at her. "Let's not forget the hippies now."

Jimmy propped his chin up in his hand, with his forefinger reaching up over his nose, as if pondering some deep question. His other forefinger tapped the picnic table.

"Now, what was that last thing you mentioned about freaks? Oh, yeah, women that can't handle their eyelashes!"

Claudette blushed and smiled. "Oh, now, Mr. Two Fingers, is that any way to treat an old lady, putting me in the same vein as them heathens?"

Jimmy slapped his leg and smiled. "I'm sorry, Claudette. I just couldn't pass this moment up!"

The crowd had gone back to its normal flow like the last ten minutes never happened. Jimmy returned to his chili and fry bread, saving a few bites and giving them to Snoop. Snoop eagerly took the last few morsels and licked around his mouth to catch any remnants.

"And might I say that certainly is a brave little dog going after the likes of Michael Senderman like that."

"Hmpph, Senderman, that's an odd name."

"Odd name, odd family, Mr. Two Fingers. Bunch of old miners from way back. I never did care for that family."

Claudette was still dabbing away at her face and adjusting her compact in her hand. "Oh, heck, this is no use. I'm gonna have to go do something about this." She rose from the table and gave out a little moan from the stiffness that had set in while sitting there. "My cousin Rena lives right around the corner. I'm gonna go see her and fix my face." She rolled her eyes. "As if that's gonna do any good."

Jimmy stood up. "Do you need any help getting there?"

"No, no, I'll be fine. Thanks for asking, and thanks for amusing an old lady on such a fine day. I do hope we meet again. I would like to hear more about this lady friend of yours. Stop in for tea later, if you see the porch light on. I do make the best tea." She put her hands towards Snoop, who was on top of the table. He walked over and licked her fingers. She grabbed his little chin and gave it a little shake. Talking to him as if he were a child, she said, "Such a brave little dog you are!"

"Good-bye, Jimmy Star Two Fingers."

"Good-bye, Claudette."

Chapter 7

J immy was once again in his usual place, alone amongst all the humanity around him. His occupation as a smuggler had forced him to keep a low profile. He didn't need anybody to be too nosy or to get too close. That could be dangerous for him, and for them as well.

The kinds of people he worked with sometimes cared about one thing during their dealings. It may be getting the money, getting it straight, getting it on time, or getting it when they needed it. The last bit, the needing it part, could be the scariest. Things were not always on an even keel if someone was desperate for cash. And, in his business, everyone knew that he always either had cash or goods. Either one would work for someone looking to beg, borrow, or steal their way out of a hole, or into one which was sometimes the case.

Jimmy knew how to stand up for himself and had created a reputation over the years that made people leery of crossing him. He never admitted, at least out loud, about filling that hole if need be. But most of his business acquaintances had somehow knew that everybody had their reasons and their ways of getting where they did. Some flaunted their conquests and flourished in the fear they instilled in others.

Then others, like Jimmy, preferred to play the cool hand with nerves of steel and wits. Yet there were still those who would try to steal from someone they knew would not call the law on them. Although in his world, the law came in many different flavors. And one of those flavors, Ringo James had just saved his ass today. He wondered what Ringo was doing in Demry, and if this was a little more than just a coincidence.

The last time he saw Ringo, they were doing a deal down South outside of Nogales. With all the border patrol in the area, they needed to make transactions as quickly and quietly as they could.

Crystal was with Jimmy on that run. They parked down a predetermined road out in the San Rafael basin, a few miles from the border. Jimmy had his feet kicked up on the dashboard and looked out at the large expanse of grassland surrounded by the low, dry mountains. A small clump of trees were far off in the distance. The grass was waving in the midmorning sun. It looked like ocean waves gently coming towards them. Jimmy imagined that this was how the East African Serengeti looked like during dry season. In his mind, he pictured a pride of lions stalking a gazelle or a zebra.

"Jimmy, why can't we ever do this in the city? Why do we always got to come out here and wait around in this lonely ass desert? This creeps me out, being out here all by ourselves." Crystal took a long drag of her cigarette, looked out the window, and exhaled. "What if there's bandits out there waiting to get us?"

Jimmy looked down in his lap as he was rolling up a joint. He smiled and said, "Sweetheart, that's exactly who we are waiting for."

Jimmy licked the paper and blew on it to dry. Handing it to her, he said, "Here, smoke this. It'll relax you."

Crystal was twisting her long blonde hair into a braid, being careful not to touch it with the head of her cigarette. "You know, I only like that stuff if we're gonna have sex, Jimmy. But hey, I'm game if you want to go in the back." She smiled at Jimmy and stroked the inside of her long tan leg.

Jimmy loved it when she wore her cutoffs. He found her to be irresistible, and it was hard for him to say no when the mood arose.

"Love to, darlin', but the boys could show up any minute now."

Jimmy knew that the quickest part of the deal was the time between when the goods arrived and when they would leave. He knew with Ringo, though, that he could be waiting for hours, even overnight, if he felt it wasn't right. But he always showed and left quickly.

Crystal napped in the back, as Jimmy scanned the road for dust or any green border-patrol vehicles. He knew that was the same thing Ringo was doing from another part of the valley. While it used to make him nervous to wait, Jimmy had come to love the cloak and dagger of outwitting the feds on what they considered their home turf. He also knew it was not as romantic or as dangerous as it may seem. It is mostly just sitting on your butt and waiting for the right time.

They kept a car somewhere in the vicinity to make the transfers, then it would be back to their bikes for the ride to wherever their home was at the time. It would usually be an older nondescript car with enough room for four or five guys and enough room in the trunk to carry the contents of the deal. In Jimmy's case, it was usually marijuana. He didn't use or like to deal in the harder stuff, even though he had the connections and could make a lot more money.

After a few hours of sitting, as the sun was reaching its peak, Jimmy saw a small line of dust a few miles off. The dust kicked in the air behind the car remained in the air for a long time, looking like a dragon's tail as it rose and set.

Twenty minutes later, a pale yellow LTD pulled up and parked about thirty yards away. Two guys got out and stood by the front of the car. Another got out of the back and opened the trunk. Then Ringo got out and slammed the door shut. This startled Crystal, and she climbed into the front seat of the van. Jimmy got out of the van and met Ringo halfway between the vehicles.

"Jimmy Star Two Fingers, good to see you again, my man. Sorry to keep you waiting, but they've been poking around a little today. Like to catch them at shift change when I can."

"Likewise, Ringo. How's things?"

"Fair to fun, Jimmy boy. You know how I roll. Ain't always fair, but it's sure always fun!" This was one of Ringo's tag lines he would use whenever possible.

Ringo looked over Jimmy's shoulder towards the van. "Who's in the van with you, Jimmy?"

"That's my old lady, Ringo."

"Why, you sly old devil. Ballsy enough to travel with meat these days! Let's have a look."

"The only thing you need to look at is the color of this money in this bag."

Jimmy handed the bag to Ringo. Ringo threw the bag back to one of his men. "Count it, Steel."

"Can't believe you still let that jackass ride with you, Ringo."

Ringo shook his head back and forth. "He is a handful but solid."

"So, who's your girl, Jimmy?" Ringo was craning his neck as he looked towards the van. Jimmy took notice of the many rings he wore on his hands. They were making small clacking sounds as he rubbed his fingers back and forth.

"Let me and the boys take a look. She sure do look good from here." Ringo's eyes got big and he began to laugh. "Come on out here, pretty lady!" Ringo shouted. "Let's have a look at you; we don't bite."

"Stay in the van, Crystal!" Jimmy yelled, not taking his eyes off Ringo. "No need for you to be out here."

"You know, we could just take her if we want. Her, the money, and the dope. Leave you out here for the coyotes."

Jimmy kept looking right at Ringo. "You wouldn't do that, Ringo. You're an honorable man."

Ringo laughed and said, "Take a good look at me. Go on."

Jimmy started at the ground looking at Ringo's silver tipped boots. He worked his way up past a pair of massive thighs to his silver scorpion belt buckle. His black leather vest had the insignia of the gang he rode with, along with a few others, including one in capital letters that just said "BRUTAL." When he looked to his head, Ringo was smiling back at him with big white teeth that shone through his black bushy beard. He was wearing sunglasses, and his head was bald and shiny.

Ringo liked to play games with Jimmy, and he knew it. But this time, he had Crystal with him, and he had to play this game a little different.

"You gonna trust me again, ha, Jimmy?"

"You have never given me a reason not to, Ringo."

Ringo looked down, spit on the ground, and shuffled his feet. "Times change, Jimmy."

"Yeah, times change, Ringo, but people don't. You didn't come all the way out here to fuck me, Ringo."

"Not you, but maybe that cute little lady you got here with you."

"Not today, Ringo. Not today. Let's do this already."

Ringo yelled back behind him. "Steel!"

"Money's right, Ringo."

The other two guys with Ringo brought out two large duffle bags and laid them on the ground behind Ringo.

"You want to check the goods?"

"No, I trust you, but I'm not gonna take my eyes off you."

Ringo kept looking at the van. "Come on out, girl. It's okay. Jimmy wants you to meet his friends."

Ringo started walking towards the van. Jimmy pulled a nickel-plated.45 from behind his back and pointed it at Ringo's head.

"Whoa, Jimmy." Ringo stopped in his tracks and put both of his hands halfway up and laughed. "Nice piece, Jimmy. Hope it's loaded.'

"Oh, it's loaded, all right."

The other men, seeing this, pulled their guns and ran towards Jimmy. Steel, the twitchier of the three, said, "Let's gut 'em and take their shit!"

Jimmy remained calm and stared Ringo straight in the eyes, even as Steel pointed a.38 snub at this head.

"Deal's a deal, Ringo," Jimmy said.

"Put your guns down, boys. Jimmy's just playing with me here."

"You sure, boss? Lets fucking off him right now!"

"Go on back to the car, Steel, and take these two with you. I'm all right here. Aren't I, Jimmy?"

Jimmy was still pointing the gun at Ringo's head. "So far, so good, Ringo. But a deal's a deal."

Ringo put his hands to his hips and let out a deep breath. "Yeah, Jimmy, a deal's a deal."

Jimmy lowered his gun and put it back in its holster underneath his Hawaiian shirt.

Ringo held out his hand. Jimmy knew there would be no trouble or double cross, and he shook Ringo's large hand.

Jimmy asked Ringo. "Why do you always have to fuck with me like that?"

Ringo let out a hearty laugh and slapped his knee. "Oh, I like your style, Jimmy Two Fingers. Like it a lot. You should ride with us!"

Jimmy had still not taken his eyes off Ringo. "You know me, Ringo. I'm a solo act."

Ringo was walking away laughing when he turned to Jimmy and asked, "You'd a shot me over meat?"

"I knew it wouldn't come to that, Ringo."

"How so, Jimmy?"

"Like I said, Ringo, you're an honorable man."

"You're too fucking much, Jimmy." He held his hand in the air as he walked away. "Adios, amigo!"

Jimmy stood in the same spot and watched the car until they drove away.

Chapter 8

That was the last time Jimmy saw Ringo until today. They had both decided separately that holding guns on each other was in nobody's best interest. The cooling off period fell away, and they both found different partners to do business with.

Jimmy put Snoop back on his leash and headed towards the music. A blues band was blasting out a standard cover that had at least the younger ones in the crowd dancing. Jimmy noticed a large tent in the corner of the park that had a banner with the German word "Biergarden" scrolled hastily across the top of it. He had thought most of the older generation who had worked the mines was mostly of Slavic descent. But for now, who was to argue with what they called their beer?

As he got a little closer, his pace quickened to meet his thirst. *It has been an eventful day for me,* he thought to himself. A breakdown, a stroll that was akin to a date, fry bread and chili, a fight, and then Ringo.

"Ah, yes, I think it is time for a few beers. What do you think, Snoop?"

Snoop was busy on his own mission following the scents of the day, at least as far as his leash would let him.

The *Biergarden* was underneath a sturdy canvas tent at least one hundred feet long. The sides were open, and men, boys, and a few women flowed freely in and out. Long tables flanked the inside of the tent. In the middle were several beer stations with young girls barely old enough to drink pouring and egging the eager men to have another one. Jimmy got two beers and juggled them with Snoop's leash to a table in the corner that was a little quieter than the commotion in the middle of the tent.

As he looked around, he noticed that the participants under the tent had sectioned themselves off. The older men were on the fringes of the tent. The younger men stayed closer to the girls pouring the beer. It was the younger group that tended to be more boisterous in their drunkenness, letting the beer get the better of their tongues and ego.

A man of about forty, with a local mine shirt on and dirty face, yelled down to him. "Hey, buddy."

Jimmy pretended not to notice until he called down. "Hey, buddy, you with the dog!"

Jimmy turned to see him and a few others tipping their beers towards him. "Hey, nice job with Mike Senderson; that guy's an ass."

"We're glad we won't be seeing him here today!" another man said. Laughter followed and they all touched their plastic cups together.

Jimmy tipped back and said, "My pleasure."

He went back to sipping his beers, staring down at the beer rings that occupied most of the space on the tables.

The man in the mine shirt spoke again. "Nobody likes the guy. He's always running his mouth off. But his uncle owns the mine or he'd probably been run out of here years ago."

Jimmy turned to them again. "Well, I guess I'll just chalk it up to doing my civic duty, but I really didn't do anything."

"Sure, you did. You stood up to him. The rest, well, the rest is just details." They all laughed and cheered again.

Jimmy replied, "The community has been served well, and I thank you for your appreciation."

Jimmy twirled his beard in his hands and sipped at his beer, while Snoop slept underneath his feet. When his second beer was almost finished, the man with the mine shirt showed up and put two more beers down in front of him. "Thanks again, buddy." And he left.

Jimmy stared again at the beer rings and thought about all the times he had spent trying to be anonymous amongst a roomful or, in this case, "tentful" of people. He usually blamed it on his occupation, where guarding your identity was a premium. But lately, he began to think it was something deeper, and his career was just a symptom of something he really didn't care to look into all that much. At times, he thought it could be either or both. But for now, the beer tasted good going down the back of his throat.

He was envious of the men around him. He thought that most of them had probably known each other for years, if not their whole lives. Together, they live, die, play, and drink. What he wouldn't do for friends like that. He at one time thought he had found a group of fellas like that. In fact, several times in his life, he bonded with different groups of guys but somehow managed to get stabbed in the back by letting himself get emotionally attached to others. "Too guarded I guess," he muttered under his lips.

Loneliness was something he often regretted, but at other times, his comfort with it came in quite useful. It allowed him the time and freedom to be where he wanted to be and when he wanted to be there. His occupation led him to unlikely associates who ran the gamut from biker to businessman to bankers, with a sprinkling of other road warriors he had met along the way.

Jimmy was often amazed at the types of people willing to get involved in the business of contraband. Your least likely suspects were sometimes the game's biggest players. Money is money in this world-most people wanted it, and your share to boot.

He noticed the beer had been taking effect when two big hands with multiple rings, some with death heads and pentagrams, were laid down before him. He looked up into the bright smile and bushy beard of none other than Ringo James.

"Jimmy Star Two Fingers! How the hell you've been, man? Mind it I sit?"

Jimmy twisted his beard and motioned with his cup to take a seat.

"Last time I saw you, you had a damn gun pointed at my head. Well, besides earlier, I mean."

"Ringo James, seems to me we were both doing a little pointing that day." Jimmy wiped his hand on his jeans and stuck it out for Ringo to shake.

"Jimmy Star Two Fingers, I've been meaning to ask you how the hell you got that name."

"Long story there, Ringo."

"Give me the short version, and I might leave you alone for the rest of the day."

Jimmy looked across the table at Ringo's hands. They were the biggest hands he had ever seen on a man. Cuts, scrapes, and bruises took their place next to the rings that adorned each finger.

"Well, Ringo, I don't much like telling that story. But I guess after today, I owe you one. Gotta tell you, though, it's not as interesting as one may think."

"Lay it on me, Jimmy."

Jimmy sighed and took a sip of beer while he brought his mind back to the day Nathan had visited him in the hospital. Beat up and bruised had never been a problem for Jimmy. It came with the territory sometimes. There was always somebody who wanted what he had. At least what they thought he had. But the two Cubans who were hell bent on taking the cash or product that he did not have had really roughed him up that day. More than his body could take. By the time he crawled out of the alley they had dragged him to, he was barely conscious. Broken ribs and a punctured lung had earned him a trip to the hospital.

Nathan had come for a visit to check on him. He brought his girlfriend Veronica with him. Jimmy had a secret shine for Veronica. Unknown to him, Nathan and Veronica could see his crush on her from a mile away. Being much older than him, Veronica thought it was sweet.

Nathan assured Jimmy that the two men who beat him would be dealt with, and that Jimmy would not have to worry about them again.

"I wasn't worried about them in the first place, Nathan. They didn't have nothing over me that I couldn't handle and were about ready to leave when I think I pissed them off."

"Why you wanna go piss someone off after they stop beating on you, Jimmy?" Veronica had asked.

Jimmy winced as he tried to sit up in his bed. "I didn't want them to think I was weak and could be pushed over again like that."

"Don't you worry about that, Jimmy. Those two would be getting theirs soon as we find them. Them two are dumb motherfuckers; they'll turn up again looking for the easy way out. And we'll be there when they do. I guarantee you that! Ain't gonna have any of my men being sent up here to the hospital without any retaliation. No fucking sirree! Not on Nathan's watch." Nathan shook his head back and forth as he held the safety bar on the side of Jimmy's bed.

"So what did you do to piss them off, Jimmy Star?" Veronica asked.

Jimmy got up on his elbows and grimaced at the pain coming from his ribs. "When I was lying there all beat up, all I could hear was them breathing heavily, and it reminded me of someone having sex. And then a bad joke came into my head that I just couldn't resist letting out."

Veronica put her hand on her hip and pointed her finger at him. "So you got all this hospital stay 'cause you told them a bad joke?"

"Uh-huh."

"Oh, I got to hear this one," Veronica said while pushing the bangs of her hair out of her face.

"You're not going to like it."

"I'm sure I'm not. Not if it ended you up in here looking like this."

Nathan crossed his arms in front of his chest and said, "All right, let's have it, Jimmy."

"So I was lying there on my side kind of doubled over, and I could see them just staring down at me. And it pissed me off. So I put my two fingers up at them." Jimmy raised his hand with his forefinger and his middle finger for them to see. "And I asked the bigger guy, 'You know why your girlfriend likes to masturbate with these two fingers?'

"He looked down at me and spit on the ground. 'No, wise guy, why?'

"'Because they're mine!'"

Veronica put her hand to her mouth and started to blush. Nathan just stood there for a moment, his mouth as wide open as his eyes, as if contemplating the whole meaning behind it. Then, after a brief moment, he bust out into uncontrollable laughter. His belly heaved in and out over his belt. He leaned over and put his arms on Veronica's shoulder. "I told you, baby, this white boy is one crazy motherfucker!"

Nathan held his own two fingers up in front of his face and said, "'Cause they're mine!" His laughter intensified, and tears started rolling from the corner of his eyes.

Veronica looked at the two of them. She smiled and shook her head. "You men are crazy; take a beating like that. I guess you did deserve it after that, Jimmy. Lucky they didn't kill you after that."

"Yeah, my timing wasn't the best, but I got in that motherfucker's head."

Nathan smiled wide at Jimmy. "Oh, you sure did, Jimmy Star, two fingers and all!"

Then Nathan stopped laughing and stood straight up. He held his forefinger in the air. "Oh, I got something here, Jimmy. Got something indeed." I been trying to think of a nickname for you for some time, and now I got it."

His big smile beamed across the room. He bent over and looked Jimmy in the eye and said, "From now on, I am going to call you Jimmy Star Two Fingers! Oh yes, it has a mighty tone to it—Jimmy Star Two Fingers."

"And that, Ringo, is how it all started. He called me that every time he saw me. And before you know it, so did everybody else. Well, everybody except Veronica. She just called me Jimmy."

Ringo crossed his arms together and smiled at Jimmy. "I always knew you were one crazy bastard, Jimmy. But that is one funny story. Almost got beat to death for telling a bad joke."

"No, not a bad joke, just bad timing."

"Bad timing indeed."

Jimmy twisted his beard in his fingers. "Nathan paid for my whole hospital stay. Said it was the least he could do since I was protecting his assets."

"Honor amongst thieves, huh, Jimmy?"

"I guess you could say that, Ringo. Nathan was good to me. He started giving me bigger deals after that. I started making a lot more money. He also gave me my first gun when I got out of the hospital."

"Do you miss those days of hustling out on the street?"

Jimmy thought for a moment. "No. I did at first. But I like what I do now. Besides, the streets are crazy now. Kids are killing each other over nothing these days."

"I hear you there, Jimmy. It's getting tougher and more ruthless all the time. Scumbags around every corner that don't give a fuck about you."

"Thanks for helping me out today, Ringo. That guy looked like a linebacker."

"Not carrying today?"

Jimmy patted his chest with both hands and reaches around to the back of his belt. "Not today. Not here at least."

Ringo sat down. "Never can tell with a guy like you, Jimmy."

"Nope, you never can, Ringo."

"Eh, anyway, it wasn't nothing you couldn't handle. I hope I wasn't stepping on your toes in front of that lady you were with. Always seem to try to embarrass you in front of your women now, don't I?"

"Seems you do, Ringo."

Jimmy smiled. He was genuinely glad to see Ringo. Despite their years of being on edge, they did seem to create a bond that was only known by them.

"So why did you jump in then?"

"First off, the guy was a total ass, and second, I got to keep my edge with my boys. Make sure they don't think I'm soft. Fucking cutthroats I run with always looking for a weakness. Keeps them on their toes."

"Anyway he fucking deserved it, pushing that old man around and treating his wife like that. He is probably home kicking his dog right now."

"I didn't think you regarded woman all that highly counting on the last time we met."

"Times have changed, Jimmy. Besides, that was mostly just my bully act in front of the boys." Ringo leaned in closer to Jimmy, resting his elbows on the table. He put his fist into his palm and rubbed the rings on his fingers. "I have been known to be a little rough with the tongue around the ladies. Mostly, though, I just feel sorry for them getting mixed up with guys like that today...and guys like you when they can go out and get a real man like me anytime they want!" Ringo's big beard shook as he laughed.

Jimmy relaxed and sat back, crossing his legs. This stirred up Snoop, who jumped into his lap. Looking across to the bear of a man, Snoop began to growl and let out a few short barks.

Ringo put up his arms in surrender. "Ho, now, little buddy. I didn't do it. Call him off, Jimmy!"

Jimmy laughed and scratched Snoop on the head. "It's his biker growl. Taught him that when he was a pup."

"She's a cute little thing now, isn't is she? Speaking of cute, is that your new girl you're with, or you still got that pretty young thing you were muling with?"

"No, it's just me and Snoop, and don't offend him like that." Jimmy picked Snoop up by the legs and swung him belly first towards Ringo. "He's a boy...see!"

"Oh yeah, real man there. Making me jealous with that thing there."

Clearly annoyed, Snoop jumped off the table, scurrying across Jimmy's lap and back onto the ground. He gave out one last little growl and curled up into a ball.

"So what brings you to these parts, Jimmy?"

"Van broke down. Needs a new water pump."

"Damn, you still driving that same van?"

"Sure thing. Two hundred thousand miles and still purring like a kitten most of the time."

"I didn't think that thing would make it out of those dirt roads we were on last time I dropped your stash off."

"Yeah, she's a sleeper. Looks like a school mom running down the road."

Jimmy smiled and Ringo laughed. "School mom my ass!"

"How about you, Ringo? You don't look like the town fair kind of guy to me."

"Oh, hell, Demry days. I try to make it here every year. My uncle used to work the mines here. Been coming here since I was a kid."

"Hmppph, I can't picture you as a kid."

"That same woman been dishing out that fry bread and chili since I was a kid, too. Worth it just to come up here for that. Also, my cousin's wife passed. Thought I'd show my respects at her funeral."

"Sorry for that."

"Yeah, shit happens." Ringo shrugged his big shoulders and looked around the tent. "Damn, I was hoping he'd come today, but if he was anywhere, he'd be right in here somewhere."

The man with the mine shirt came over, carrying a tray. He put down two beers in front of both of them. "Thanks again for putting Mike in his place today."

Jimmy held up his cup and cheered Ringo. "Anyway, thanks for helping me out today. You didn't have to do that."

Ringo got up and said, "Makes no sense to me watching an old mule get kicked around. Never know. Might need you again someday."

Ringo handed Jimmy a piece of paper, and he put it in his pocket.

He held out his hand and they shook. "Good to see you again, Jimmy Star Two Fingers. Catch you around the block. Keep it fair and fun now."

"Yeah. You, too, Ringo. Keep 'em wheels side down."

Jimmy watched as Ringo walked out of the tent. With his back to him, he raised his fist. "That's right. Wheels side down."

All the men, including the young ones, made room for Ringo as he walked out of the tent. From Jimmy's viewpoint, it reminded him of the parting of the Red Sea.

Chapter 9

He drank his last beer down slowly, avoiding any direct contact with anyone else. The cool dark tent contrasted the bright afternoon light. Jimmy walked through the park, stopping at a few booths along the way to admire the works of the local artists and craft makers. The large cottonwood trees throughout the park reminded him of a place his dad used to take him outside one of the army bases where they had briefly lived.

It had been almost ten years since his dad had passed, and Jimmy didn't like to think about it much, if ever. He didn't see or talk to his father much in the last half of his life. Their falling out had been enough to make the wedge that had been driven since childhood stick for good. Although Jimmy would have liked to have a closer relationship with his father, he could never come to forgive him for what he had done.

Once Jimmy was old enough, he joined the Army, following in his father's footsteps. After boot camp, he was assigned to the 115th Forward Support Battalion in Fort Hood, Texas.

He thought it would be so cool to be part of such a large organization that he had grown up in. He knew what all the medals, badges, and insignias stood for, and what each of the units responsibilities were. But he had always felt like an outsider, being raised in what he called Army Foster Care most of the time.

Since his mother died, and there was no one to watch over him while his father was on duty or deployment, he would get passed from family to family. He would rarely be with one home for more than three months before being moved to a new base, or a new family.

Joining himself when he turned eighteen seemed the most natural thing for him. He considered it an honor to serve his country and be with a new group of guys whom he hoped to be lifelong friends with.

Boy, was he ever wrong. Wrong time. Wrong place. Wrong leaders. Wrong group of guys. Jimmy was deployed to his first conflict twelve weeks out of boot camp. At first, he was excited to be deployed. But that excitement turned to sorrow and heartache, as part of his job was to load flag-draped caskets onto cargo planes for their long journey home.

No matter how proud or loyal these servicemen were to their unit and their country, they were still dead. Jimmy felt so bad for the families they would be flying home to as dead men. No parades, no reunions, no college, no new dreams, no new cars, no homes—just a box and a one-way trip to the cemetery. Sometimes he wished he could take their place.

His morale was low, and the other men in his unit shunned him and called him names like "pussy" and "loser." His commanders told him he should toughen up, "It's wartime, son. Buck up, soldier, and do your job."

Jimmy had wanted to be a lifer, and the men in his unit would laugh and say, "Lifer, you probably won't make it through next month!" One of the biggest loudmouths in his unit, Corporal Timothy Owens, crossed Jimmy's line early one morning when he told him, "Yeah, we hear your dad was a pussy, too. That's why you moved around so much. Nobody wanted him either."

That was the first time Jimmy ever hit a man with the intent of causing serious harm. By the time they tore Jimmy off him, the damage had been done. A broken jaw and a crushed eye socket landed Jimmy in the brig and eventually got him a dishonorable discharge.

Jimmy's dad, Colonel Star, was devastated at the news that his son had beaten another soldier half to death. As much as he never saw his dad that often, and sometimes for long periods of time, he loved his dad and looked up to him. He was all Jimmy had, and no one was going to disrespect his only family in front of Jimmy Star. Especially Corporal Owen, whom Jimmy thought was just a loud-mouthed punk, anyway.

When Colonel Star flew in to see Jimmy in the brig, their impromptu homecoming didn't go as well as Jimmy would have thought. Colonel Star demeaned his son, as if he were just another serviceman. "You've brought shame and disrespect to your uniform, your unit, your commanders, and the Army. And you have brought shame to our name and our family."

He was in no way condoning Jimmy's actions for sticking up for his father and his family. "There are other ways to resolve a disagreement, Private."

Jimmy found this bit of advice to be quite ironic since they were in the middle of a war.

Chapter 10

Once stateside, Jimmy went to stay with a distant aunt until he could get on his feet. His father had given him just enough money to buy a bus ticket and nothing more.

On the bus ride, Jimmy wondered what he would do in Omaha. The question was answered quickly by a step uncle whom he had never met before today.

"I'll tell you what you're gonna do. You're gonna get a job and keep your nose clean!"

Jimmy kept to his room, which was not much bigger than a closet with a bed and a bureau. The only time he would see his aunt was at suppertime.

He spent his days looking for work. But nobody wanted to hire an out-of-town kid who had a dishonorable discharge. Jimmy finally found work as a prep cook for a cafeteria for the local slaughterhouse employees. The plant ran twenty-four hours harvesting pigs. Jimmy hated the word "harvesting." It reminded him of what the Army had done to him. Groomed him, recruited him, harvested him, and then spit him out into the world.

The hours were long and hard. The pay was pathetic. But he liked a few of the guys he worked with, and they became friends. Before long he was sharing a house with a few of his buddies. The place was a shabby little cottage overlooking the railroad tracks. He shared a bedroom with Mick Taylor, who grew up in Omaha. Mick liked to drink rum and smoke pot, lots of pot.

Jimmy soon grew to like the shenanigans of living in a party house with other guys his age. After about a year of just buying bags of pot and smoking them, they decided they should start selling it. At least enough to cover their own stash. An old rule of dealing soon came into play, 'Don't deal what you do, especially when everyone else is doing it.' Within a few weeks, instead of enjoying smoking with his buddies, they were all in competition with one another trying to sell the same stuff to the same people. This led to fights and accusations between them. The peaceful environment had grown distrustful and vengeful.

Before long, Jimmy got caught trying to sell a bag of pot to one of the cooks where he worked. He knew he had been set up. Not only did they fire him, but they took him away in handcuffs. He spent three weeks in the county jail. No one, not even Mick, would come to bail him out.

Finally, the judge let him out on his own, but he would have to be back in a month for court. When he got back to his house, he found that all of his belongings had been hastily piled on the back porch. His clothes and other belongings had been rained on and were strewn with trash and beer cans. Jimmy wanted to hurt someone really bad but refrained, considering the consequences of last time.

His room had been rented to someone else. His roommates claimed they had been told that Jimmy ratted them out, and they were now out of business until things cooled down. They needed to rent his room to cover the rent, or they would have all been out on the street.

Jimmy looked to Mick, whom he considered to be his close friend. Mick wouldn't look him in the eye, and he bowed his head down.

"Oh, so this is how it's gonna play out—leave me out in the street cold and broke like that! I see how it is. Too scared to man up for yourselves, so let's take it out on Jimmy Star." Jimmy pulled a knife from a kitchen drawer and stuck it in the wall.

He looked at each one of them. "If you see me walking down the street, turn the other way. If you hear me coming up behind you, run—or you might end up like this wall, motherfuckers!"

Jimmy pulled the knife from the wall and dropped it on the ground. He rummaged through the kitchen and found a garbage bag. On his way out, he took one more look at Mick, who immediately dropped his head and said, "I'm sorry, Jimmy. I'm sorry about all of this."

Jimmy collected his belongings and put them in the bag, and then he started walking down the street. His anger turned to sorrow as he stood under a large oak tree, in the muted light of a streetlamp. He yelled at the sky, "How could all of these families all around the world have all of this love and togetherness, and I can't even have one friend? Why, God? Why?"

Jimmy carried the sack to the only place he could think— his aunt's house. It was dark inside when he knocked at the door. His aunt looked out the window and quickly came out to the porch, closing the door behind her.

"Jimmy, what are you doing here?" She held herself in her night coat against the chill of the evening air.

Jimmy's voice cracked. "Aunt Ellie, I need a place to stay."

"Oh, Jimmy, I'm so sorry. You can't stay here. Your uncle Frank works at that plant, and everybody there knows what happened. And, well, it's just not right getting mixed up with those people and selling drugs. Your father is so ashamed."

Jimmy snapped at her. "You told my father?"

"Of course I did, Jimmy. He asked me to look after you."

Jimmy clenched his fist open and closed. His throat began to close on him, as all he wanted to do was moan or growl. "You shouldn't have done that, Aunt Ellie!"

His aunt watched his fists as they opened and closed. She didn't know what he would do and became afraid. After all, marijuana users were known to become violent. Jimmy watched her as she took a step back away from him.

Jimmy turned and put his hands on the railing, staring out into the hazy night sky. "It's not like you think, Aunt Ellie. Not like you think at all...I...I...I was set up."

His aunt felt a little more at ease with his back turned to her and not posing any direct threat. Her shrill voice spoke up a little louder this time. "Set up? Set up for what? Are you telling me you didn't do it?"

Jimmy looked down at his hands that held a death grip on the railing. He knew he was about to be turned away again this evening, and he had no idea where else to go.

"It's not like it's a big deal, Aunt Ellie."

"Well, it's a big deal to us. We can't be having a known drug dealer living with us. If they find out down at the plant, who knows what could happen. Frank could lose his job. Then we would all be out in the street."

Jimmy found it odd that his actions were perceived and tied to everybody else being out on the street.

"A drug dealer. I'm telling you, Aunt Ellie, it's not like that. It was just a little grass. Come on, this isn't nineteen fifty; it's all over the place."

"Yes, I suppose it is. Thanks to the likes of you and your friends. The police report stated that you were selling an illegal drug."

Jimmy turned to her, shocked that she would go as far as requesting a police report. "You read the police report?"

She shrugged and looked on the floor. "W...w...well, I didn't—but your uncle Frank did. He was gonna bail you out when we heard you were in trouble, but when he found out what you did, he turned round and left. Said you should...well, never mind what he said."

Jimmy could only imagine what his overly obsessive and uptight uncle said about him. He stood there staring at his aunt, wondering what it would be like to live with a man who planned every second of their day and decided that she should have few thoughts left to her own.

She lowered her voice again and stepped towards him, taking both his hands in hers. "Jimmy, I am so sorry things have turned out the way they have. I really am. But we can't let you stay with us. We just can't."

She lowered her head again and began to shake it back and forth. He put his arms around her shoulders, and she put hers around his waist. "I understand, Aunt Ellie. I'm sorry to put you in this position."

"No, I don't think you do understand, Jimmy. It's not easy turning away my kin, especially after the life you have had. It's hard on me, Jimmy. It's breaking my heart to see you like this and knowing there is nothing I can do."

Jimmy shivered in the cool Omaha night. His clothes were damp from sweating, and he asked if he could take a blanket with him.

She came back with a blanket, a few sandwiches, and an old backpack they had stored in the cellar. She was crying. She gave him one last hug. She told him not to come back; it would cause too much difficulty with Frank. She went inside, shut the door, and turned out the porch light.

That would be the last time anyone would put their arms around Jimmy for a long time. He stood in the dark for a few moments, looking at his belongings. He sat on the front porch step, ate one of the sandwiches, and looked at all the streetlights and all the porch lights. In each one was probably a mother and a father serving nice warm meals and helping with homework. Some would have a little dog to play with.

He began to cry. It came out softly, as he would not allow himself to totally let it go. After he ate another sandwich, he left the porch. He promised himself that he would never cry again. And he never returned to his aunt's house.

Chapter 11

The judge gave Jimmy a one-month suspended sentence and told him he didn't want to see him back in his court again. "It's fine men like yourself that allow themselves to be taken over by drugs that breaks this court's heart every day."

When he left the court, he didn't know where he was going, but he was definitely getting the hell out of Omaha.

He hitched a ride to St. Louis. Before long, he was peddling pot out on the street corners. But it didn't feel right to him. There has got to be a better reward for risking his freedom. That's when he met Nathan.

Nathan taught him the ropes and ins and outs of the business that he called moving contraband. After a few months of grooming, Nathan asked Jimmy if he wanted to be one of his long distance drivers. "Only thing is it gets lonely out there being on the road by yourself all the time."

That was music to Jimmy's ears.

"And don't get no notions. I know people all across the country get you cut quick if you start getting notions of your own. Understand me, Jimmy?"

That was when Jimmy was a young man getting started in all of this. Now, he had his own connections and contacts. But his heart was still frozen. He had had a few flings and short romances, but it is hard to commit when you are on the road. Hardest thing for him to remember, though, was that he did have a heart somewhere deep inside. But he did forget, and it stayed stuck inside, until he met Crystal.

Chapter 12

Jimmy and Snoop, his little Chihuahua, were on one of their usual routes southeast of the Prescott between the people's valley and the middle of damn near nowhere. It was close to being totally in the middle of nowhere, except there was still the resemblance of a road, and they were on it. Considering his occupation as a smuggler of illegal contraband, particularly marijuana, Jimmy preferred the anonymity of his Dodge Astro van and the quiet back roads of Arizona.

The late afternoon sun was glaring on Jimmy's windshield, but in the distance, he could make out a car with its hood up, and smoke was coming out of the engine compartment. "Shit, Snoop, you know how I don't like doing this, but I'm gonna pull over and see if I can help." If he was heading north, he would have kept going. But seeing his load was only cash for now, his nerves were relaxed enough to see if he could help a fellow traveler before nightfall.

Jimmy knew all of these back roads, front roads, and side roads from the Mexican border north to Jackson Hole and from San Diego to West Texas. He had carved out routes where others didn't even know there was a road. That was part of his game and his work. And it was unlikely there would be much traffic down this road once it got dark.

The faded blue sedan looked empty when he pulled up behind it. He made sure he left plenty of room between the two. "Well, Snoop, this may be for naught, but let's give it a look see."

Jimmy tucked his snub nose 38 behind his belt and pulled the tails out of his Hawaiian shirt out of his belt to conceal it. The car was still smoking as he got out of the van, and he could see liquid forming a puddle on the side of the car. It looked as if no one was around as he approached the car, until he saw a pair of feet sticking out of the rear passenger window.

He had learned from trial and error not to walk up roadside if he could help it. He had had one too many close encounters with vehicles straying his way while the driver was rubbernecking.

Hmm, and a woman's feet to boot. Well, well, this could be interesting. As he slowly approached the window, he wrapped his knuckles on the trunk of the car and yelled out, "Hello."

He did not want to get to close in case that pair of feet were not alone. He had known it to happen that when a couple's car broke down, they can tend to get a little frisky out of boredom or just plain old need. A woman's head popped up; her face was covered in long blonde hair. When no other head joined her, he approached the window.

The woman was pulling her hair back from her face when Jimmy looked in. One glance was all it took for Jimmy to know he was in trouble. She was by far the most gorgeous woman he had seen in quite some time, and definitely the prettiest encounter he had ever had during a breakdown. Her long tan legs were sticking out from a pair of cutoff shorts frayed at the ends, sending streaks of white cotton down her upper thighs. A small tank top graced her athletic body. When she looked at him, her soft brown eyes were forever seared into his. His heart, that had been so guarded and closed suddenly leapt into his throat and opened wide when she smiled and said, "Hi, I'm Crystal!" He choked on his saliva and began to cough uncontrollably. Jimmy leaned over and pounded at his chest to try and stop. But he couldn't stop. *Some impression this is making, Jimmy,* he thought to himself.

Crystal got out of the car, and, with a hint of concern in her voice, asked, "Are you all right, sir?"

Between coughs, Jimmy said, "Don't call me 'sir.'"

"Well, maybe if you put your hands up in the air like this." Crystal stretched her arms up over her head, causing her tank top to hike up over her belt buckle and expose her lean stomach and belly button. Seeing this, Jimmy swallowed another load of saliva and continued his gagging and coughing.

Crystal held her hands to her head and asked, "Mr. whatever your name is, are you all right?!"

Jimmy continued to cough but leaned up a bit and held up his forefinger."

"Okay, then, you can stop anytime now. You're making me nervous."

When the coughing didn't stop, he held up the peace sign to her.

"Okay, two fingers." Crystal began shaking her upper body up and down, and then touched him on the shoulder. "Does that mean you are all right? Oh, what can I do to help?"

Now Jimmy thought he was indeed in heaven hearing her say his name. Now if he could just stop coughing long enough to introduce himself, he might be okay.

"Mister, what the hell are you doing here? Did you come out here just to let me watch you die? 'Cause if you did, I don't want nothing of it!"

Jimmy calmed down long enough to tell her, "I'm here to help."

"Help! Sounds more like your gonna keel over on me."

Crystal spoke with a short slight Southern accent, the kind that Jimmy adored, at least what he could hear between his coughing and wheezing.

She looked to the sky, shaking her head back and forth. "Lord, is this some kind of a joke? I asked for help, and this is what you send me! Well, for tarnation's being, I thought you liked me."

Jimmy started laughing, and it made him cough again, but at least this time he was able to settle down. "Girl, you're killing me here."

"Me!?" She turned her head quickly towards him. She took a step back and put her hands on her hips. "Looks like you're doing that just fine on your own."

Jimmy finally composed himself long enough to introduce himself. He gave a slight bow and put out his hand. "Jimmy Star Two Fingers, how may I assist you?"

"Assist me? First off, I ain't shaking your hand until you wipe it off with something. And assist me?" she questioned with a shake of her head. You can barely stand up. How are you gonna assist me?"

Jimmy wiped his phlegm-covered hands on his pants and asked, "And you might be?"

Crystal put her hand to her chest and looked him in the eye. "I might be?" she asked. "I might be digging your grave if you don't pull it together. That's what I might be."

Jimmy finally stood up all the way and cleared his throat. "Oh, you're too cute, girl. What I mean is what's your name, sweetie?"

"I thought I told you my name already. But in case you didn't get it, my name is Crystal, Crystal Ann Delocoix. And I'm from the great state of Alabama."

Crystal leaned back against the car and pulled out a pack of Pall Malls. She lit one up and handed the pack to Jimmy. "You want one of these, Mr., uh, Two Fingers, did you say it is?"

"Uh, no, thanks."

"Good. The way you cough, one of these might put you over the edge." Crystal gave out a short laugh with her mouth closed. She blew out a long smoke ring and asked, "What'd you say your whole name was again?"

"Jimmy Star Two Fingers at your service."

She repeated his name slowly. "Jimmy Star Two Fingers. That's an odd name. Is that Indian or something?"

"No, my given name is Jimmy Star. The two fingers part got added on a long time after that."

She looked at him confused. She scrunched her shoulders. "Added? Better be a long story behind that long name. You didn't give yourself that name, did you?"

Jimmy put his arm up against the car and leaned next to her. "Nope, not one bit."

She looked up at him from beneath her blonde bangs and asked, "You swear?"

Jimmy laughed. "Yes, darlin', I swear."

Crystal put her elbow in her hand and took another drag and blew it in his face. "Now don't you go *darlin'* me either. You sure ain't known me long enough to be calling me darlin'!

"You ain't gonna go start getting all creepy on me, are you? Guy stopped by here a little while back. Weasely little fella, I tell you. Bad teeth and smelled like he been drinking turpentine. Got all creepy right away. Starts telling me how we should run off together and start a family. Called me pretty and all, but I know that already. One little compliment don't want me getting all up with a stranger and start making babies. Some men, I tell you—I don't know what they must be thinking—see a girl and get all googly and shit."

Jimmy had never heard a woman who could talk so fast and smoke the same time.

"He started getting all close to me and tells me he's gonna kiss me."

Crystal took another drag, reached into her front seat, and came out holding a long-barreled.45 half the size of her arm. Jimmy took a step back and put up his hands.

"Told him neither me nor Bessie here wanted to be kissed by a man as ugly as he was. I pointed old Bessie here right at his balls and told him he best be on his way lickety-split fore either me or Bessie got mad." She laughed and looked at the gun shining in the late afternoon sun. "I tell you, Mr. Two

Fingers, when he saw old Bessie here, I thought he was gonna darn near pee his pants! He high-tailed it out of here right quick without another word." She swung the gun around a little. "Yep, ol' Bes here has got me out of a few scrapes. That was about the last car I remember coming by this way. But then I must have fallen asleep back there. Being this hot, it sure made me tired."

Crystal was waving the gun around as she talked, as if it were not in her hand. Jimmy took two fingers and pushed the muzzle away, so it wasn't pointing at him.

"So what's your story, Jimmy? You do want me to call you, Jimmy. The others all cute and all, but I like Jimmy."

"Sure, Crystal, Jimmy will be just fine."

"What brings you down this godforsaken road in this dry, dusty, dull place?"

"I happen to think the desert is quite pleasing this time of the day."

"Yeah? What's so nice about it?"

Before expounding on the virtues of the desert, Jimmy tried to erase the fact that Crystal was the most beautiful woman he had ever seen. And the fact that she had a cigarette in one hand and was waving a long-barreled .45 in the other just set his heart off to the races, and he wanted to tell her so. But her escapades with the last lonely traveler made him think he should be a bit more prudent. At least for now.

Jimmy looked out over the horizon and took in the views. He looked north towards the Date Creek Mountains. Being early May, the chollas and barrel cactus were in full bloom. The soft petals of the prickly pear flowers were still hanging on to their leaves. The towhees, sparrows, and chickadees were darting in and out of the low oaks and the junipers that had spilled their bounty of berries to the dry desert floor. The smell of the creosote and oak hung in the soft breeze. Jimmy took a deep breath, and, with a long sigh, he let it out, "Ahhhhhhh...."

"Take a deep breath, Crystal, and look around. Ain't no place prettier than this in heaven. At least until you get a little farther down to the Sonoran. Now there is some pretty land."

Crystal looked at him and asked, "The who?"

"The Sonoran." Jimmy laughed.

"Uh, what's a Sonoran?"

"Oh, I'm sorry, the Sonoran Desert. It's a different desert south of here."

Crystal put her hand on her hip. Her eyes got big. Cocking her neck forward, she looked at Jimmy as if he were nuts. "You meaning to tell me you people down here separate out your deserts one from the other?"

"No, it's not like that. They are just different temperate zones."

Crystal shook her head at him and rolled her eyes. "Y'all spend too much time in the sun baking that old noggin' up there, making you a little cuckoo! And don't you be looking at me like I'm dumb now. I took two years of junior college fore I ever met the likes of you or that other crazy fella we run off earlier." Crystal pointed the barrel of the gun straight up and held it out in front of her face. She blew out a smoke ring that split when it reached the barrel. "Ain't that right, Bessie!"

Jimmy stepped to the side a bit, not wanting to be anywhere near the barrel of the .45-caliber. Holding both arms up, he asked her, "Do you mind putting that thing away, please? You're making me nervous."

"No problem, just as long as you keep yours tucked right where it's been, too."

Jimmy looked at her like he had been caught with his hand in the cookie jar.

"That's right. I'd seen yours, too. Hard not to miss when you were all coughing and flapping around like you were."

"Deal. I'll keep it right where it is. If it makes you more comfortable, I will go put it back in the van.

"No, Jimmy, no need for you to be doing that. I'm guessing if you wanted to shoot me, you'd have done it by now."

Jimmy crossed his arms. "Now, Crystal, why would I want to shoot a sweet young lady like yourself?"

Crystal took one more drag of her cigarette, blew it out, and dropped it on the ground. "You mind stomping that out for me, Jimmy. I don't want to put my boots on yet." Crystal put the gun back on the front seat and tossed a blanket over it. She scrunched up her cheeks and pursed her lips. "So, Jimmy, do you think you can help me out?"

Chapter 13

J immy leaned into the engine compartment, while Crystal
looked in over his shoulder. It did not take him long to
determine that the engine had major problems. Oil and
antifreeze were leaking from the head gasket and block. A
trucker roared by, laying on the horn and blowing Crystal a
kiss. She replied by giving him the finger.

"I swear, Jimmy, what is up with men when they are out
on the highway? Turn into children, I tell you. Acting all
cute and brave, blowing by at sixty miles per hour. You'd
think they had never seen a girl before." She shook her head
and lit another cigarette.

Wiping his hands with a rag, Jimmy told Crystal that her
car had most likely blown the engine and was not going
anywhere.

"Can you fix it?"

"I'm afraid, Crystal, that even if we could get it to a
garage, it probably can't be fixed. I think she's done for."

"Shit, shit, shit, shit, shit!" Crystal stomped around in
circles and pushed her hair from her face. She put her head
inside the engine compartment. "You sure you can't fix it?"

"Oh, I'm sure. You see, I think your camshaft froze, and—"

Crystal cut him off. "My what froze? How the hell does anything freeze in this weather? God, I used to think it was hot in Alabama." She wiped her brow with her forearm. "What am I gonna do now? Not even a goddamn Seven Eleven around here for a girl to get a cold pop. You ain't got one, do you, Jimmy?"

"I might be able to do you one better, Crystal. How 'bout a cold beer? You're not driving."

"Oh God, I'd love a cold beer! That's the other thing I asked God for. Send me help and please bring me a nice cold beer."

They leaned up against the trunk of the car, longnecks in hand. Crystal was smoking, and Jimmy was staring off into the mountains some distance from here.

"So where was it you were heading, Crystal?"

"Well, I am heading to San Diego. I was gonna go surprise my cousin Ellen, who lives out there. I needed to get the hell out of Alabama. I dropped out of college and was spending my time doing stupid stuff and wasting all my money on my dumbass boyfriend."

"Why didn't he come with you?"

"He thought it was more important to be partying down at spring break than to tend to his very own girlfriend. So I took his car after he left and got out of there."

Jimmy took a long draw on his bottle and shook his head. "So, I take it he doesn't know you have his car."

"Nope. Not yet. Should be figuring that one out pretty soon, though, when his hangover wears off and he goes home."

"Oh, Crystal, I like your style, girl! But you're not going to get to California in this car."

"Damn, Jimmy, I don't know what to do."

"Well, I could get you down to Wickenburg. Maybe catch a bus from there. But that won't be until tomorrow, and it being Sunday and all, you might have to wait until Monday."

Crystal slouched and looked around. "You'd do that for me?"

"It'd be my honor, darlin'."

"Okay, since you're giving me a ride, I guess you can call me *darlin'*. Then she wagged a finger in his face and smiled. "But don't go getting creepy on me. No hanky-panky lessin', I say so. I'll be keeping Bessie close by, just in case."

"Okay, no hanky-panky lessin', you say so. Girl, you crack me up!"

Crystal put her beer and cigarette on the trunk and turned a cartwheel. "Woo hoo! Well, then, what's the plan, Jimmy Two Fingers?" She picked her cigarette back up and chugged down the rest of her beer. "Any hotels around here or good places to eat?"

Jimmy pointed towards his van. "Welcome to chez Two Fingers, the finest hotel and restaurant within fifty miles of here."

Crystal eyed the front of the van, making note of all the splattered bugs and dirt that covered the grille and windshield. She frowned and looked at Jimmy, and then back to the van.

"That's it?"

"That's it for tonight, darlin'."

When she looked back at the van, Snoop jumped up on the dashboard and wagged his tail. Crystal's mouth flew open and turned into a huge grin. She put her hand on her chest and turned to Jimmy. "You didn't tell me you had a dog!"

"You like dogs?"

Crystal took a deep breath and looked to the sky. She clasped her hands together and said, "Thank you."

"Uh, something you should let me in on, darlin'."

That was the other thing I asked God for today. You see, I like to ask in threes, in case he doesn't hear the first two."

"Well, what did you ask him?"

"I told him I wished I could snuggle with a dog tonight."

Jimmy cleared his throat and made believe he was straightening out a necktie. Crystal punched him softly in the arm and said, "Not that kind of dog, silly!" She pointed to the van. "That kind of dog, the kind with four legs."

Jimmy yelled to the van and pointed his thumb towards Crystal. "Snoop, you're gonna owe me for this one, little fella." Then he looked into Crystals eyes. Her smile melted his heart. "Yes, he's gonna owe me big time."

Chapter 14

The late afternoon brought with it cooler temperatures and thinning crowds. Most of the older folks and families were gone now. The line at the beer tent, while still healthy, had taken a turn down. As Jimmy walked by, it was still raucous as forty stories were being blurted and repeated over stale beer breath and equally stale ears.

Jimmy took a step towards going in, then turned and walked by. It was much too late to catch up with the vibe that was going on inside. A walk through the park led him back to main street. The stores were open a few hours later than normal today in hopes of increasing their till. It would be months until the holiday season, and the merchants would use this weekend as one last chance to boost sales.

The restaurants were full of patrons. The stores all had their doors open. Many were adorned with balloons, ribbons, and flyers gracing their windows, giving this otherwise dull and run-down street a more festive atmosphere.

The next block down looked like it had plenty of saloons attached to its sidewalks. Looking through the windows, Jimmy could see shoulders hunched over beers, as if guarding them from unknown marauders. Conversations took place in mirrors and over pool tables.

He looked at these and many others he had pulled into over the years as ports in a storm of boredom and loneliness. A place where men and women could be as anonymous or as friendly as they liked. A place where unlikely friendships were born on the same eternal yearning most of us have—to be together or a part of something larger than ourselves.

Jimmy decided that the Elks Club would be his next port of call. An old man was smoking a cigarette on a wooden bench that served as sentry by the front door.

He looked up at Jimmy. His glasses were crooked on his nose, but he didn't seem to mind or even know they were. "Are you an Elk?" the old man asked.

"Yes, I am. Been a member of the Elks for twenty-five years or so."

Nathan, out of all people, had turned Jimmy on to the Elks Club. He had told Jimmy that if you're gonna be a traveling man, you should have a membership to the Elks. "See, Jimmy, a fella can find a friendly place for a couple of beers without some asshole wondering and getting all up in your business. Some of them even got food. But don't ever park too close. Park a few blocks away. All the local police are keeping an eye on them cars and trucks that are parked there more than a few hours. Don't think they don't take notice, 'cause they do!"

Jimmy had asked if he should be worried about someone stealing his car if it was parked too far away. "First off, Jimmy, you always want to make sure that your stash is secure. Many ways to do that by making compartments in and around your vehicle that nobody knows is there. Second is you place toggles underneath your dash that are connected to the ignition. You have to have the toggles switched in the right sequence or the ignition won't work. Someone breaks into your car, they'll be gone the minute they find it don't start."

"Sit down, young fella. I want to ask you something." Jimmy sat next to the old man. His hands shook as he brought the cigarette to his mouth. He looked to be in his eighties. His thin body was topped with a head of equally thin hair combed back on the sides. His grey button-up shirt was stained from neck to belly down the button line. He had a light windbreaker, blue khakis, and pull-on shoes. One of his heels looked to be about three inches thicker than the other. He looked at Jimmy's hand that was holding the leash.

"Is that a dog you're holding?" he asked loudly.

"Yes, that's my dog."

"What?" the old man shouted back, squeezing his face together and moving his head closer to Jimmy.

Jimmy spoke a little louder. "I said, yes, that's my dog."

"That sure is a tiny dog. What's your dog's name?"

"His name is Snoop."

"What?" the old man said again.

"His name is Snoop."

The old man took another drag from his cigarette and rested his arm on his. "That sure is a funny name for a dog."

"Well, he's a funny dog."

The old man stared straight ahead while licking his lips and asked Jimmy, "So did you have a nice Christmas?"

Jimmy realized the man was lost in the grips of more than just a few beers. Much worse than that, obviously, Alzheimer's or some other affliction had taken place sometime over the man's lifetime. But somehow he had made it to this bench on this day, and despite probably not knowing where he was, seemed to be enjoying himself.

"What's your dog's name?"

Jimmy leaned in close to his ear this time. "Snoop. My dog's name is Snoop."

The old man turned to Jimmy and straightened his glasses. His mouth hung open as if he couldn't believe what he had just heard. "Poop? Why would you name your dog Poop?"

Jimmy put his hand to his mouth and laughed into his fingers, trying not to embarrass the old man.

The old man dropped his cigarette to the ground. He looked down at it and tried to stomp it out with his oversized heel, missing on all attempts. He sat back up and clapped his hands down in his lap. "Fuck it. It won't be the first time this town has burned down. So, did you have a nice Christmas?"

Jimmy went along this time. "Yes, I had a nice Christmas. Did you have a nice Christmas?"

"What?"

"Did you have a nice Christmas?"

"Why are you asking me about Christmas; it's not Christmas. It's Demry days."

Jimmy's shoulders drooped. He was hoping this condition was not in store for him.

Two men came out of the door. Both appeared to be in their late forties or early fifties. "Okay, Pop, time to go home."

The bigger one asked Jimmy. "Is he out here chewing your ear off?"

Jimmy looked apologetically at him. "He's trying."

"Yeah, I know Pops is getting old."

"I know I'm getting old. You don't have to rub it in," the old man said.

"Party's over, Pops. We've got to get you home before Mom starts worrying about you."

He grabbed his father by the elbow and helped him up. The other brother told Jimmy, "He still remembers Demry days, though, and insists on coming down to the Elks for a beer. He's been doing it for sixty-eight years, and he hasn't missed one yet. Other than that, he doesn't remember much."

They both grabbed an elbow and lifted him up. He brushed them off at first, then held one of his son's hands for balance.

"Take care," Jimmy said.

"Yeah, you too," the brothers said.

As the old man shuffled away, he looked at his younger son and said, "That man's got a dog named Poop!"

Both sons burst out in laughter. The younger son told his father, "Oh, Pops, you crack me up!"

The last thing Jimmy heard as they walked away was the old man blaring, "What?"

Chapter 15

Steel asked Ringo that night. "Why did you stick up for that old Two Fingers today? Hell, last I remember, he was holding a gun to your head. Made you look like a fool."

"Oh, Steel, that's why you are where you are at, and I am where I am at. He didn't make me look like a fool. He held his ground and showed me the respect I deserved."

Steel scratched his head and looked down at the bottom of his glass of beer.

"Funny thing about holding a gun on someone, your finger gets a mind of its own when it comes to pulling the trigger, and nine times out of ten, it doesn't get pulled."

"So why do think he didn't pull it that day? You think he was scared?"

"That guy, scared, not on your life. The way I see it is he knew you guys would have killed him, grabbed his girl, and done unspeakable things to her."

"So why didn't you shoot him?"

"Me, I like a guy who has the balls to stand up for himself. That and a deal is a deal, and we had a deal."

Steel tilted his head back and let the last of his beer flow down his throat. He nodded to the bartender and pushed his glass towards him.

"You should have let him get his ass kicked, mouthing off to that dude like that."

Ringo put his big arm around Steel's shoulder. "Steel, my man, you are as tough as nails, but you sure do have a lot to learn about people."

Steel spit on the floor. "Think we'll be doing business with him again?"

"Who knows? I hope so. Two Fingers is one solid dude."

Steel pushed Ringo's arm off his shoulder. "Should've kicked his ass myself."

The bartender brought down two more beers. Steel immediately slammed his down, while Ringo just took a sip.

"Let me tell you one thing, Steel. You would be doing yourself a favor to think twice about crossing him. The man has got a cold heart. Loners like him don't usually last too long in this business, but he has been around a long time. Didn't stick around all these years by being soft."

Ringo took another sip of beer. "But something was different about him today."

"Yeah, what's that?"

"Not sure yet, Steel. Can't quite put my finger on it yet. Hell, maybe he is just getting old."

Chapter 16

J immy decided that a port in the storm may not be in his best interests tonight. Perhaps a stroll to see where the mechanics' garage was would be in order.

An hour later, after walking up and down through several nice older neighborhoods, Jimmy found the industrial side of town and came upon a garage constructed of cinder blocks and painted white. The faded black lettering over the two garage bays said, "Gus & Son." Gus nor his son were anywhere to be found. Several vehicles of various size and shape were parked in the lot next to the garage, waiting their turn at a trip inside.

Jimmy made note of the address and went along on his way. Snoop enjoyed this part of town. It was obvious, by the way he dragged Jimmy from pole to pole, that the canine population was alive and well on this block.

Jimmy came to the end of town. The street from here would loop back around towards main street and the park. There was a cut log on the corner wide enough to use as a seat. Jimmy needed to give his knee a break, and he stopped for a rest. Candy wrappers stuck in the fence waved behind him like small flags. It smelled like dog piss and old cigarette butts. Nothing new for Jimmy, though. Life on the road had led him to many places like this.

The crescent moon was beginning to peek through the night clouds. The crickets had begun their chorus, and Jimmy could see bats chasing their nightly meal around the one light pole that shadowed over the corner. The air was cool, but not cool enough for a jacket.

He looked back on the day's events and decided that it just couldn't have been a coincidence the way it all turned out. No, something was at work behind the scenes here. That something was still behind the veil.

Jimmy got back to his van a little after 8:00 p.m. The street of mostly two-bedroom brick houses was very quiet. The porch light was on at Claudette's house, as well as one dull light from behind a curtain. He knocked on her door. She answered the door free of makeup and wearing a pair of slippers and a housecoat. Her hair was in a scarf. There was one more day to go for Demry days, and after her run-in with mascara today, she wanted to look her best tomorrow.

"Why, Mr. Two Fingers, nice to see you again."

"I hope I'm not disturbing you. I wanted to ask if I could park my van in front of your house for the night. He pointed his thumb over his shoulder. "I've got everything I need to sleep and clean up."

Claudette's eyes beamed, and she gave Jimmy a wink. "Couldn't stay away, could you? I knew you were still around and was hoping you'd make it back this way."

"You do have a way about you that is rather irresistible." Jimmy smiled. "So, is it okay if I park it there?"

"Nonsense, pull it in the driveway." Claudette looked up and down the street. "No need to give these old fuddies around here a reason to call the police. And believe you me, they would if they see you crawling in and out of your van in the middle of the night. Bunch of old uptight codgers I got surrounding me. I tell you, scared of everything, except their own righteousness.

"I guess we can keep up the ruse if you really want to get them talking."

"Ruse or no ruse, honey, believe you me, they are already talking."

"Well, I thank you kindly."

As Jimmy was walking away, Claudette called to him. "Mr. Two Fingers, I did just put on a pot of tea if you'd like to join me when you get settled. Oh, and bring that little dog of yours, too. I'll be up for some time. Sleep is one of those glorious things we tend to lose as we get older. I guess the Lord is trying to give us extra time to make up for the things we set out to do. Problem is he took the body away while he was at it. Oh, Mr. Two Fingers, he does get it backwards sometimes."

Jimmy came back in accompanied by Snoop. When he let him off his leash, he scurried around, sniffing all of the corners and furniture. Claudette's kitchen was plain and had a round wooden table in the middle and lattice-back seats that were in need of dusting. Plaques, awards, and pictures of family adorned the walls.

Claudette was pouring tea when she noticed Jimmy looking at the pictures. "Most folks put the pictures of their families in the parlor. But I spend most of my time in here, and I do hate to eat alone." Claudette sat next to Jimmy and inched her seat closer to him. "Oh my, it has been some time since a younger man has come calling on me, isn't this exciting?!"

Jimmy blew into his teacup and took a sip. He winced and pulled his head back from the cup. "Whoa! Now that's a cup of tea. What the heck did you put in there?"

Claudette produced a small bottle of rum from her housecoat pocket and showed it to Jimmy. "Gives it a little flavor now, wouldn't you say?"

"It sure does, Claudette. You can keep these things coming!"

"Oh, goodie!"

The pale yellow room looked like a throwback to the times he lived with his aunt many years ago. The handles on the fridge were faded chrome and looked like they would be happy resting on a Buick somewhere. The stove had sleek round corners and big knobs that had their numbers worn off them from years of use. The neatly laid tile on the floor was black and white checkerboard. The back window was open, and a soft breeze was blowing a white laced curtain slowly along the bottom of the window sill. He felt like this is what his mother's kitchen would look like if she were still alive. The crickets chorus was only interrupted by the occasional dog bark that would perk little Snoop's ears.

"Well, my Mr. Two Fingers, that certainly was an exciting day! You and that biker fella are the talk of the town. People are just buzzing about Mike Senderson being put in his place." Claudette put her cup down and looked at her pictures. "That poor wife of his, though, has to put up with that man night and day."

"I couldn't stand to see that poor woman crying any longer. If I was a little younger, I'd of taken him out by the collar like a trash bag."

"Lucky for you those bikers came by when they did. Saved you the trouble. Tell me, though, Mr. Two Fingers, right before all the commotion, you were speaking of some woman who was in your life."

Jimmy sat back in his chair and let out a deep breath. "Phew, I guess we were."

"Tell me something about her then. Was she your wife?"

"No but if I was smart, I would have asked her. I'm sure she is married by now."

"So where did you meet this woman, Mr. Two Fingers."

Jimmy thought back fondly to that day he saw those two feet dangling out of the window. "Well, I helped her out one day when she was broken down, and it just sort of stuck."

"What stuck?"

"We stuck—stuck together like Siamese twins for the next two years."

"And then what?"

"Then we became unstuck."

"That's too bad when that happens. Seems like couples these days find more reasons to not be together than to stay together. Couples these days just don't seem to have the glue that they used to. Back in my day, divorce and family breakups didn't happen that often. But now...." Claudette's words trailed off as she looked at the pictures of her husband on the wall. "Well, now, things are different. Such a tragedy what's happening between men and women these days. Everybody thinks it's all about happiness all the time."

"Well, isn't that the way it's supposed to be, Claudette?"

Claudette took a sip of tea and put it back down. "This is the way I see it. Happiness is a short-lived thing. Oh, sure, it can come and go, and that's what gives it its balance. Me and my husband didn't always get along. How could we? We were two different people living two separate lives. You don't always mesh all the time. That's no need to throw the whole thing out now, is it?

"Trouble is, now, the way I see it, everybody always trying to build one happy moment after another. That's all fine and dandy until things go wrong. Then they haven't had the practice to go back to in the bad times to figure out how to make them work. There has got to be a balance in there somewhere, wouldn't you agree, Mr. Two Fingers?"

Jimmy stared into his teacup and blew little circles into the dark liquid.

"All the young people now just working on that thrill-a-minute. They look at us old folks here like we don't know what hell we were thinking. Think were just all living in the past."

Claudette gave a long sigh before continuing what was turning out to be a rant. Jimmy sat quietly, hoping it would come to an end long enough to get some more tea.

"But we're here every day just like they are. Sitting and thinking, and eating and breathing just like everyone else!"

Jimmy noticed her slur becoming more evident and wondered how many cups of tea she had had.

"Once everyone got all caught up in this happiness thing, it seems everyone became more unhappy. Another one of the Lord's great mysteries." Claudette looked at the ceiling and made the sign of the cross over her chest. "Oh, forgive me, Lord. Sometimes I just don't understand."

"Amen to that, sister. Often don't know what to think of it myself. That was part of the problem with me and my girl."

"Let me ask you something, Mr. Two Fingers." Claudette cooed and wiggled her shoulders. "Oh, how I just love to say that name—Mr. Two Fingers. It just sounds so, I don't know, Western. Like being in a John Wayne movie." Claudette held up her cup. "Howdy, ma'am, like to introduce you to my riding partner, Mr. Two Fingers."

Jimmy shook his head back and forth. "How many of those things have you had today, Claudette?"

"Oh my, seems like they are making my brain a little flush. I guess this is one of those happy moments!"

Jimmy raised his cup and they cheered. "Here is to the happy moments!"

"Funning aside now, Mr. Two Fingers"—Claudette leaned in close to Jimmy and looked him right in the eyes— "what would you do if you saw her again?"

Jimmy hunched his shoulders and let out a big puff of air from his cheeks.

"I guess...I guess I'd say, 'I'm sorry. I'm a bonehead for leaving you on the side of the road.'"

Claudette looked sternly at Jimmy. "You mean to tell me you let that woman out on the side of the road!"

"Well, it wasn't like I had much choice now, Claudette. She went storming out of there, telling me to fuck off!"

"Now, excuse me, Mr. Two Fingers. I haven't known you that long, and I shouldn't be judging, but you are telling me the woman you loved just got dumped out on the side of the road like a dog!" Claudette's voice rose, bringing Snoop running into Jimmy's lap. "For Christ's sake, you wouldn't do that to your own dog, would you?"

Jimmy was too embarrassed to answer.

"After the way you stuck up for Mrs. Senderson in the park, I thought you were a better man than that." Claudette crossed her arms and gave him a sideward glance. "And here I am serving you tea makes me a complacent...uh, comparant...uh...." Claudette could not think of the word, but Jimmy knew what she was looking for.

"Accomplice?" Jimmy said.

"Makes me an accomplice just having you sitting here."

Jimmy could tell the rum was really kicking in now, as her words became more slurred and her eyes were getting fuzzy and glazed over. But the verbal beating she was giving him was not unlike the ones he had been giving himself for the last five years.

Nathan's voice crept up inside of him.

"Five years! You been carrying that grudge against yourself up inside yourself for five years! No wonder you ain't getting none. Broken hearts don't feel so bad as long as you pick it up and dust it off."

But Jimmy hadn't picked it up and dusted it off. It laid right there on that spot on Route 81, where he had left it, right next to the two Saguaro cactus by mile marker 84. Every time he drove that route, he tried not to look but always slowed down a bit, anyway. Perhaps a whiff of her hair was still lingering in the air, or it was all just a bad dream. But this thought always passed, just like the mile marker.

Claudette poured some more of her special tea and added a little extra shot in Jimmy's cup. "You can probably use this more than I can, Jimmy Two Fingers."

"Oh, Claudette, sounds like you're a little beyond a snootful."

She smiled. "Maybe two snootfuls I think."

"Yeah, maybe two snootfuls."

"Lookee here, I'm sorry I got so angry with you. It's really none of my business. But leaving a woman all alone like that, it must have scared the bejesus out of her."

"Oh, I'm not so sure of that. Not much scared Crystal. She knew how to take care of herself."

"Well, did you at least go look for her?"

"Sure did. I thought she was just blowing off a little steam. I got about a half mile down the road and turned around to go get her. But when I got back, she was gone. I looked all through the desert around there. She just wasn't there."

"Didn't she even come home to get her things?"

"The van was our home mostly. We didn't stay in one place or another too long."

"Soooo," Claudette's words were getting longer. "She didn't have a place to look for you, and you didn't have a place to look for her."

"Claudette, I've been looking for her ever since that day. I've traveled every road around here for a thousand miles just hoping and praying that one day I would run into her in a store or a diner or something. But no luck."

"Luck, you don't need luck. Sounds to me like you need a miracle."

Jimmy felt a shiver run up and down his spine, and he twitched his neck. That old familiar feeling of his heart putting on its armor was upon him, and he knew he would be ending this conversation soon. But before the flicker of hope and forgiveness totally darkened, Jimmy apologized to Claudette for not being the man she thought he was.

"Jimmy, what's in people's past doesn't always stay there. Seldom does. And I hope you can forgive yourself as I already have."

Jimmy crawled into his van. He listened to Snoop licking himself to sleep. He reached under one of the shelves he had built and opened up the compartment. He reached in where he kept one the scarfs that Crystal used to wear around her head. He held it to his chest, and then put the scarf up to his face, trying to catch one more scent of her hair or perfume, but he knew it had long since faded away.

He breathed in deeply one more time. "Please, God, just let me smell her hair one more time."

It surprised him that he was asking for "otherly" help, as he hadn't asked since the night on his aunt's porch. But the times were changing, and he knew that deep inside he was, too. Twenty years ago—heck, even ten or five—he knew that the conversation he had just had with Claudette would not have taken place. He would have shut it out completely. But now, despite the armor, there was still a spark that smoldered there waiting to burst into flames. He just hoped it wasn't too late for him.

Nathan's voice came to him again, repeating one of the many lessons he had taught his young apprentice. "Jimmy, it ain't never too late for nothing, except dying. Then you just dead. Other than that, anything is possible."

Chapter 17

Jimmy's usual routine of smoking a joint in the morning was cut short when Claudette appeared at the side of his van. She had a cup of coffee in one hand and a dog biscuit in the other.

"Well, look here, Snoop, a treat." Snoop's ears perked up from the mention of his name, and he clambered onto Jimmy's lap.

Jimmy rolled down the window, "Morning, Claudette."

"Good morning, Mr. Two Fingers. I almost forgot I had these in the back of the pantry. Does your little dog like treats."

"Well, sure he does."

Claudette handed Jimmy the mug. "Hope you like cream and sugar."

"Yes," Jimmy said, pulling the hair back out of his eyes. "Like it sweet, sweet like you."

"I'm afraid I wasn't so sweet to you last night. Sticking my nose in your business." She swept her hand around the neighborhood. "Like these people here stick their nose in mine. Good Lord, I tell you, it terrified me this morning thinking I'm getting more like them all the time."

"Maybe you've been like them for longer than you think, Claudette."

Claudette leaned her elbow against the van and put her hand to her cheek. "Maybe so, Mr. Two Fingers, maybe so. But my tongue does tend to loosen a bit more than normal when I start drinking my nighttime tea. Whoo!" She let out a big burst of air. "But I do apologize if I butted in too far. Anyway, your past is your past, just as mine is mine."

"Apology accepted." Jimmy watched the steam rise from the mug. He blew into the cup and asked, "This isn't special coffee, is it?"

She slapped him lightly on his arm. "No. Just coffee this morning! Anyway, I'll have some breakfast up in a bit. You're welcome to come join me and use the shower and such."

"I feel like that would be imposing on you."

"Nonsense, Mr. Two Fingers. That's where our generations end. We don't let a little old disagreement spoil the whole party. We keep on going for the better of both. Besides, today is the town picnic. Finest day to be in Demry. Even the likes of Mike Senderson get on their best behavior today. Wear something nice."

"Sounds like an invitation."

She looked up at him. Her age showed through her skin. "You think?", she said.

"Well, thank you. So what do you think your neighbors are going to think of a strange van in your driveway?"

Claudette took a sip and coffee and said, "I don't give a rat's ass what they say. I already seen them peeking out of the corner of their windows this morning. I may be old, Mr. Two Fingers, but my eyes are sharp."

Claudette looked around the neighborhood. "I see them peeling their blinds back and taking the long view hunched in their corner. Ain't no spine left in this neighborhood, I tell you. If they don't like it, they should yell across the street, or do the proper thing and come knock on my door and ask me what the hell is going on!"

Jimmy sat back and mused at the small town's injustices.

"My cousin Rena got three calls already this morning asking what this van is doing my yard."

"Why don't they just call you?"

"I guess I've been known to bully up on them, and they are just scared of me. Imagine that, scared of me." Claudette shook her head back and forth, staring at the ground. "Seventy-two years old and I can barely walk down the street without getting winded, and they're scared of me. Hmph."

"Oh, Claudette, I get the feeling this is going to be one of those days!"

Claudette smiled back at Jimmy and winked. "They always are, Mr. Two Fingers. They always are!"

Chapter 18

The atmosphere was quite different at the park today. The hot temperatures of yesterday had subsided on a cool breeze. The beer tent and stage were gone, as well as the artist and food booths.

Most of the people were dressed as if they had just come from church. It being Sunday, many probably had. Collared shirts and dresses were the norm today. Jimmy had dug out his Western style white collared shirt, adorned by a turquoise bolo. He wore a pair of tweed pants and cowboy boots. He even broke out his prized Stetson hat for the occasion.

"My, my, my, you do clean up well. What a handsome man you are, Mr. Two Fingers."

"My father told me a long time ago that I should travel with at least one set of nice clothes. So this is what you get."

"I tell you what, Mr. Two Fingers, you may not find the woman you are looking for, but you are sure to raise the interest in some of these single ladies around here. I might even have to borrow that cane of yours to beat them off with!"

The cane today was more of an ornament, as Jimmy did not think he would do much walking, and his knee was feeling much better.

All of the picnic tables were lined up end to end in the middle of the park. Jimmy wondered where they kept so many tables. A bluegrass band was playing softly on one end of the tables, and all of the food tables were on the other end.

The massive amounts of food on the tables made Jimmy start to salivate. Everything he could imagine to be at a picnic was probably somewhere to be found here, including two pigs on a spit. The grills in the background were laying layers of flavors all over the park. Workers, all dressed in red, white, and blue aprons, were busy making the last-minute preparations before the festivities would begin.

Jimmy had to do a double take when he looked across the park and noticed Ringo. He was not wearing his signature leather vest, belt, jeans, and boots. His attire for the day was a collared polo shirt tucked into a pair of khakis. Despite his casual attire, he still looked as tough and fierce as he is.

He was with a group of men and women that Jimmy assumed were members of his family. His usual entourage was nowhere around. The circle of people he was with went around one man in particular. A small line of people lined up to give him a hug or shake his hand.

"That's Billy Simpson," Claudette told him from behind. "He lost his wife last Wednesday. The funeral is tomorrow. I am so glad he came to the picnic today. It'll do him good to be around folks that love and respect him. He is a good man."

Jimmy looked on in sorrow and jealousy. Even in death, these people had a connection that he had rarely, if ever, felt himself.

Jimmy's aversion to settle anywhere in particular came from far back in his youth, and he never let go of it. Watching the goings-on in the park, he thought it might have been nice to settle down somewhere with Crystal and have some community and family around them. But these feelings only came up after she was gone.

Somewhere in the back of his mind, he pulled up an image of the two of them years ago at an associate's house north of Taos, New Mexico. They were sitting in the backyard on an old swinging bench, watching the sunset over an endless sky. Crystal looked so sexy that day in her cowboy boots and cutoff jeans. Her long blonde hair was flowing out from beneath her cowboy hat. Jimmy swore to himself that he would do just about anything for this woman.

He had asked her if this was a life she wanted. "Jimmy, I'm just happy to be with you here today. Sure it would be nice to have a house with a yard and a kitchen, regular showers, sleeping in a regular bed, watching TV on a couch, and all that other stuff most folk get to do."

"Yeah, that stuff."

"Sure I would, wouldn't you?"

Jimmy never answered her question. His inability to commit or even consider a path other than the one he was on was not something he was ready to face. Not then, and not now. But why not? He shook his head and let his daydream drift away.

With full plates, they headed to a table. Claudette was flanked by two of her cousins, Ella and Rena. The laughter and chitchat started as soon as they saw one another and had not stopped even for a minute.

The sun twinkled as it drew its bow across the strings of leaves of the Cottonwood trees, leaving a trace of early autumn color cascading down on the hungry, happy crowd underneath its canopy.

The meal started with a proclamation from the town's mayor and a prayer from one of the local chaplains. The various religions in the park listened attentively, and all ended with amen. The plates and conversations ebbed and flowed as the meal went on.

The picnic went on for hours, and Jimmy felt less out of place, all the while meeting Claudette's cousins and other friends and family members. But he couldn't help himself from looking over at Ringo. He just found it so odd that the both of them were here today in this setting.

As the pig, potato salad, pickles, and coleslaw-laden plates turned to cookies, cake, and coffee, Jimmy made his way over to Ringo.

Ringo introduced him simply as Jimmy Star to his family members. They exchanged handshakes, and Jimmy passed on his condolences to them.

Ringo moved to the end of the table. "Have a seat, Jimmy."

Jimmy sat across from him, almost laughing at the way Ringo was dressed.

"Well, don't you make quite the cowboy?! Didn't barely recognize you either there, pardner."

Ringo dug into a piece of blueberry pie a woman had brought over for him. "Thank you, Aunt Ellen."

"We are all glad you made it, Steven. It means a lot to us."

Jimmy waited until his aunt had left and leaned across the table. "Steven, how's it going, Steven! Talk about a double take. Collared shirt and your name is Steven!"

"Well, Jimmy, I'm sure you weren't born with the name Two Fingers attached to the end of it either, so there you go."

"Got me there, Ringo."

Ringo looked up. "That's better. Only the older ones call me Steven anyway."

"Where's your crew today?"

"Sent 'em back on their way. Sunday's family day, and then we got the funeral tomorrow. No need for them to be here; this ain't their scene."

"I bet they'd get a kick out of you in that shirt, though."

Ringo looked down at his clothes. "Oh, these? These ain't no big deal. It's Sunday, and these are my people. I've got no need to stand out in front of them while I'm here. Matter of fact, it's a nice break to blend in a little bit."

A small girl in a blue plaid dress, knee-highs, and pigtails came running up to Ringo. She was crying and trying to say something in between her sobs.

"What's the matter, darling?" Ringo said while pushing her hair back out of her face.

"Uncle Ringo, Joey pushed me down and said I was stupid."

"Well, come here, honey." Ringo lifted her onto his lap. She kept her head down and sobbed. "We'll take care of that little Joey later, but you're not stupid, honey."

She kept sobbing and Ringo took her into his arms and urged her to calm down. Ringo looked at Jimmy and motioned with his eyes to Snoop.

"You like doggies, Lisa?"

His young niece nodded as Jimmy lifted Snoop onto his lap.

"He's a funny looking dog, isn't he?"

She nodded no, then yes.

"How about a little piece of pie?"

She let out a small tight-lipped grin on her young face and pulled her hair back away from her mouth. Ringo fed her a little bite of pie.

"There, there. Now that's better, isn't it?"

Lisa nodded and dried her eyes with the backs of her hand.

"Now, you go tell Joey if he picks on you again, Uncle Ringo's gonna put him in a bear hug and not let go."

A smile bloomed from her cheeks, and she pulled gently on Ringo's beard. "Thanks, Uncle Ringo!"

"You betcha, honey. Now you tell Joey I got my eye on him."

She bounded off his lap and ran out to where the other children were playing.

"You're pretty good with kids, Uncle Ringo."

"That's my brother's daughter."

"I never picked you as a guy that liked kids, Ringo."

"Sheez, Jimmy, kids are easy compared to the guys you and I work with. Besides, I got four of my own at home."

Jimmy's jaw about hit the top of the table, and his eyes bulged out. "No shit, you got four kids?"

"Yep, oldest one just started college last month."

"I...I...I never knew that."

"Well, Jimmy, we never did hang out in the same room long enough to get around to that, did we? And when we did, families weren't on the top of the topic list."

"But how do you do what you do and have a family? I don't get it. It just doesn't match up."

"What!? Outlaws can't have families?" Ringo put his big hands down on the table and looked Jimmy straight in the eyes. "Jimmy, I do what I do because I have a family. Kids gotta eat and be clothed." Ringo looked around the park. "Be honest with you, Jimmy, I don't see how all these people with regular jobs do it. It's expensive having kids these days. You try feeding four kids. Damn near nothing left at the end of the day!"

Jimmy twisted his beard. "Interesting," he said.

"Ain't nothing interesting about it, Jimmy. A man has got to make his money and support his family. And, at the end of the day, guys like you and I make out a hell of a lot better than most of these folks do."

"Yeah, I believe that."

Ringo's head snapped to the side, and he pointed to one little boy. "Joseph James," he yelled, "you leave those girls alone before I come out there and get you!" He pointed quickly again when the young boy looked at him. "I'm watching you."

"But why do you keep doing what you're doing if you got kids and a family? Face it, you and I have been known to hang around some pretty rough guys."

Ringo finished his pie and took a sip of coffee. "You see, Jimmy, when we got into this game as younger men, it was for the fun and adventure, and this is how we paid for our lifestyle. Now it's my job. And what about you, Jimmy, is it your job or your lifestyle?"

"I guess it's a little bit of both, Ringo."

"Now don't get me wrong, Jimmy. I think muling is one hell of a way to make a living, and you guys make me a lot of money. But you got to start looking at where you want to be five, ten years from now. You still wanna be running up and down these roads by yourself? For a lifestyle!"

Jimmy sat silent while Ringo went on. He felt like he was getting lectured, but also considered it good advice from one of his peers.

"Face it, Jimmy, we ain't getting any younger, and the game ain't getting any easier. We just know how to do it better than most. But it ain't forever, Jimmy. Nothing's forever." Ringo wiped the crumbs off his shirt and out of his beard. "You got my number, Jimmy. I got safer things going on now for guys like you and me. No need for you to always be the lone ranger out there." He got up from the table. "But for now, it's my turn to watch the kids."

Jimmy tipped his hat. "Thanks, Ringo."

Ringo walked away, then turned back. "Jimmy, you told me something once that I haven't forgotten."

"What's that, Ringo?"

"You told me people don't change. Remember that?"

"Yeah, I remember."

Ringo touched the collar of his shirt. "I'm not so sure about that anymore."

Chapter 19

Jimmy walked the perimeter of the park dragging Snoop along. It seemed Snoop had been fed snacks along the way, and he was not that interested in the local scents.

Jimmy sat on a bench by the playground where a few dozen children were busy being children. He'd wondered what it was like for a child to grow up with the same kids throughout their lives.

The children barely noticed him. But one little girl of about five or six came over and stood closely to him in her long jean dress and pigtails of blonde hair, as if waiting to be invited in. He recognized her as the girl from yesterday, with the star painted on her face.

She wiggled her fingers at him and said, "Hi, mister, can I play with Snoop?"

Snoop's recent apathy disappeared at the mention of his name. His ears perked, and his little tail brushed the ground.

"Oh, you remember his name now, do you?"

She held her hands together in front of her, palms out, and stretching them at the knuckles. "Yep, I like that name. It's funny." A bright smile crossed her small teeth.

"What's your name, little one?"

She cocked her head slightly. Her hands were still folded in front of her. "Abby."

"Oh, that's a nice name. As long as your parents don't mind, I'm sure Snoop won't mind."

Jimmy let out a little extra leash, and Snoop ran towards the child. She got down on her hands and knees, and when Snoop got close, she shouted, "Boo!"

Snoop quickly changed directions. Abby rolled on her back, laughing out loud. Snoop came back to her, and she flipped him over and began to rub under his chin. Snoop lay there, twisting his head back and forth, looking at Abby and enjoying her playfulness.

Jimmy sat back with his legs crossed and his arm up on the back of the bench, amused at the two of them playing in the grass. "I think he likes you, Abby."

She looked up at Jimmy from under her pigtails. "I like him, too. His tummy is so soft."

"It should be after all the snacks he has had today."

"Abby pulled his legs up over his head and rubbed him up and down his stomach.

A tall woman with a floppy hat that covered her face and wearing a jean skirt like Abby's came walking over. "Why, Abby Star Delecoix, what are you doing?"

Jimmy's heart froze the instant he heard her voice. This could not possibly be real. Jimmy looked up. He still could not see her face under her hat, and her hair was much shorter. But it was her.

Her cheekbones glistened in the sun as she tilted her head, and her smile shone brighter than any star he had ever seen. She hadn't looked at him yet, and he wondered if she would run or pass out when she saw him. But much like the first time he saw her, he was stunned at how beautiful she was. And from the way his heart was beating, he wondered how or why he could have ever let her go.

"Abby, are you terrorizing this poor man and his dog? What'd I tell you about being so friendly with strangers."

Abby was still on the ground, twisting Snoop into unnatural positions. "This is Snoop, Ma. Can we get one like him?"

Crystal froze at the mention of Snoop's name. She looked down at the dog, and then to the man sitting on the bench. Jimmy lifted the brim of his hat, so she could see his face. She held her jaw half open and lifted her hat from in front of her eyes. Her knee buckled a little bit, and she took a small step back.

"Hello, Crystal."

She was shocked. She took a few quick breaths and put her hand to her heart. "Jimmy Star Two Fingers, is that really you?"

Jimmy loved the way his name sounded rolling off her tongue.

Crystal took another step back and almost tripped over Abby, who was still twisting Snoop into strange contortions.

"Watch it, Mom! You almost stepped on me!"

"I...I...I can't believe it!" she said half stuttering as her lips started to quiver. "I...I...I thought you were dead."

Crystal stood staring at Jimmy in disbelief that he was really here sitting in front of her. Jimmy raised his palms to his sides and extended his arms away from his body.

"In the flesh; not dead yet!"

"Well, stand up there, Jimmy! Didn't your daddy teach you to stand up when a woman walks in the room!" Crystal put her fingers to her mouth and looked around the park. "Well, I guess we aren't really in a room, and that's right, your daddy never did teach you much on manners. Just something you should have learned along the way. I mean who don't stand up when a pretty girl comes walking up to them?" She nodded her head out towards the park. "Other than them ol' geezers over there. But I don't think they can stand much longer than it takes to take a good pee every now and then. But I suppose you are catching up to them."

Jimmy's smile grew wide. He was always amazed at how quick the words could come out of her mouth. She moved towards him and stopped. She put her hand to her mouth and took a quick breath that almost sounded like a hiccup. Then she came forward and put her arms around him, lifted her head, and kissed him deeply on the mouth. Jimmy's head was swirling. Surely, this was a dream.

She pushed back and stood there with her hands on his elbows. Her breath was shallow and quick. She looked towards the ground then back up at Jimmy.

"I can't believe it's you." Her eyes looked up and down at Jimmy. "Take off your hat."

Jimmy took off his hat and tossed it on the bench.

She let go of his elbow, wound up, and punched him squarely on the jaw! It wasn't the hardest punch he had ever taken, but it was a good wallop. He didn't ask what it was for. She grinned and put her hand to her mouth. "Oh my God, I'm sorry, but I've been wanting to do that for years!"

Crystal leapt at him and put her arms around his, pinning them to his side. She buried her face into his chest. He looked down at Abby, put his hands out from the wrists, and shrugged his shoulders. "Momma's a hugger; she gives the bestest hugs!" Then Abby went back about her business with Snoop.

Jimmy looked down to the top of Crystal's floppy hat. "You always make a habit of clobbering guys in front of your daughter?"

She put her head so far into his chest he felt like she was trying to peek at his backbone.

"Believe you me, you're not the first man she has seen me raise a hand to. I'm not afraid to lay a licking out to a man should he be deserving of it. Nuh-uh, no reason for me to be hiding it from her, Jimmy. I don't hide anything from her, never will."

Crystal's soft Southern sway was an accent he had long missed, and he had nearly forgotten how pleasing hearing her voice was to him.

"And, by the way, Jimmy"—she looked up at him—"she's our daughter. Not just mine, yours too, the two of us."

Jimmy pulled his fingers through his long hair and leaned back against the bench using his other hand to steady himself. "Well, now, how the hell did that happen?"

Crystal crossed her arms. "Biology, Jimmy, plain and simple. How'd you think it would happen? I ain't Mother Mary. Ain't no Immaculate Conception; no angel's been flying around me."

Jimmy sat back on the bench. His heart had taken another twist somewhere between cool and hot, as he felt the beads of perspiration beginning to cling to the back of his neck. It was his turn to stutter. "I...I...mean...h-h-how? W-w-when—?"

Crystal cut his sentence off at the pass. "Plain simple facts, Jimmy." She pointed at Jimmy. "You..." She pointed to herself. "...me." Then she held her hands out far in front of her stomach, simulating being pregnant, and pointed to Abby. "Her."

"Are you sure?"

"I'm damn sure, Jimmy! That's how God made us. It's the only way I know that this thing happens: man plus woman equals baby!"

"No, no," Jimmy lowered his voice. "Are you sure she's mine?"

Crystal gave a disapproving tsk-tsk and crossed her arms. "Course, I'm sure she's yours. A woman knows who the father of her baby is. At least the women I know. Don't you think I know who I been with and when? I see that's still your biggest problem, Jimmy: questioning a woman's motives! You ain't got no reason to be assuming it's someone else's child now, do you?"

Jimmy spoke in a soft voice. "I just didn't know. I...I...I mean a baby? Me a father?" Another swipe of his hair and, indeed, the sweat had not just made its stand on his neck but was also gathering its forces along the front of his brow.

"No reason for you to be keeping your voice down, Jimmy. Long as there's a dog down there, she'll just stay down there all day. As a matter of fact, I'm gonna join her." Crystal got down on the grass next to Abby and took off her floppy hat. Her hair was short, cut just under the shoulder. But it still held the shine and beauty it always had.

Crystal put her face close to Snoop. "Snoop, Snoop, remember me?"

Snoop began licking her neck and ears. Both of the girls were laughing. "Snoop likes you, too, Mommy!"

Crystal looked at Abby. Their faces were almost touching. "Me and Snoop have known each other before, sweetie."

"Before when, Mommy?"

"Before you were born, honey."

"Can we bring Snoop home, Mommy?"

"Snoop's not ours, honey. You'll have to ask Snoop's dad."

"Mister, can we bring Snoop home with us?"

In that split second, before he answered, Jimmy's heart freed itself from its heavy armor. His dream seemed to be unfolding before his very eyes. Unlike all the roads he had ever been on, he didn't know where this road would lead him. And it was a road he was terrified and eager to explore. What had started as a Sunday picnic was quickly turning into a life-changing afternoon. Hell, he didn't even know if she would have him, but he wasn't going to let love and the chance and hopes for a family slip through his grasp without at least giving it a shot.

"I guess if your mom says it's all right if we can come by for a visit."

Crystal looked up at Jimmy, smiling. "Oh, yeah, it's more than all right, Jimmy Star Two Fingers. Much more than all right."

"Oh, goodie!" Abby got up and ran in circles. Her pigtails helicoptering out from her head.

Crystal got up and kneeled in front of her daughter. "Come here, sweetie. Momma's got to tell you something." Abby stopped spinning and stood in front of her mom. Crystal wiped the bangs out of Abby's eyes and put her hands over her shoulders.

Jimmy had never witnessed anything as soft or touching as he had in that moment. Was this what it was really like to be in love with a child, a woman, or a family? He watched as Crystal's fingers waved her bangs away from her eyes, and then she put her palms softly on each of Abby's shoulders.

"You see, this man here?" They both looked up at Jimmy and kept their eyes there for a moment.

Jimmy wondered how his armor could drop so quickly. It didn't seem fair. If he had only let himself.... He let that thought go and watched the love that was unfolding before him.

"Yes, Mommy, that's Snoop's daddy."

"Well, yes, pumpkin, that is Snoop's daddy. But you know what else, pumpkin?

Abby hooked her small finger on the inside of her mouth. "What, Mommy?

"He's your daddy, too."

Abby looked up at Jimmy and back to her mother.

"He's your daddy, Abby."

Jimmy was shocked out of his silence and began to cough. He beat his chest, as if it were a culprit leaving with his stash. He could not believe Crystal had just told Abby that he was her father. But he was not surprised. He knew that Crystal had not held a secret her entire life. Whatever came into her mind came right out of her mouth. No filter whatsoever. But this time, this was big. He kept on choking and sat on the bench.

"See you still get worked up there, huh, Jimmy?"

Jimmy didn't know what to do or say. In his life, he had faced down the biggest bikers, the meanest cops, prison guards, outlaws, drunks, junkies, pushers, and posses. But when Abby pointed her finger at him and said, "He's my daddy," well, Jimmy had never been so scared in his entire life. Nor had he ever been so in love.

"Mommy, you told me my daddy was in heaven."

"I know, sweetie. I thought he was. But God let him out to come visit us."

Poor Abby looked so confused. She hung her forefinger from her lip and looked back and forth between Jimmy and Crystal.

"Is he gonna go back?"

"Go back where, sweetie?"

"Back to heaven, Mommy."

"I don't know, sweetie."

Crystal shook her head back. "I don't know. Are you, Daddy?"

Jimmy stood in silence. He had never been put on the spot like this before.

"Why don't you go ask him, sweetie."

Abby came over to Jimmy and tugged on his pants.

"Mister, are you gonna go back to heaven?

"Jimmy's armor had completely washed away. He didn't know what to tell her, and he finally stammered out. "Well, I don't know, Abby. Sometimes God calls me back to help him."

"Well, if he does, can we keep Snoop down here with us?"

Jimmy touched her on the side of the face and hair. Her skin was so soft against his rugged hands.

"Of course you can, sweetie."

Abby jumped and did a half circle in midair. She turned and hugged him around the neck. "I'm gonna get a doggie! I'm gonna get a doggie!"

Jimmy laughed and wiped the perspiration from his brow with his shirt sleeve. He felt like he had dodged a bullet. Crystal picked up Abby and held her on her lap close to Jimmy.

"Good one, Jimmy. Playing God's right-hand man. Didn't know you two had become so close?"

Crystal put Abby back down. She scooched closer to Jimmy and kissed him again. Jimmy let her tongue swirl in his mouth, catching his breath when he could. She put her leg across his lap and put her head on his shoulder. "I thought you were dead, Jimmy."

"Why'd you think I was dead?"

"Something I heard. I tried to figure any way I could to track you down. I'm sorry I ran off like that. I know I'm stubborn and all. So I ran into this guy that said he heard you got killed in a deal down in Texas. I cried for months, Jimmy, months."

"Jimmy buried his nose in Crystal's hair and held her tight. Her fragrance brought back everything he had missed about her, and then some.

"Oh, Crystal, nothing like that ever happened. I'm still indestructible."

"I know. That idiot was probably just trying to get in my pants."

"Well, I'm here now, baby. I'm here. I still can't believe you just told Abby something like that."

"You mean the truth."

"Well, I wasn't suggesting that you lie to her."

"What are you suggesting then, Jimmy?"

"I don't know. I mean, uh...."

"Look, Jimmy, save it for the band. That little girl is my light and my soul. I never lie to her, and I never will. She's gonna grow up knowing the whole truth about her momma. And maybe, if you stick around long enough, she'll get to know something about her daddy, too."

"I never wanted to leave you, Crystal. It was just that I didn't know what I was getting into."

"Jimmy, I never meant to be hard on you, and I'm sorry if I am being hard on you now. I really am glad to see you. I used to dream of this day, Jimmy. You'd come blazing into town and sweep me off my feet like the first time I met you."

"Boy, we did do some sweeping, didn't we?"

"We sure did, Jimmy."

They sat holding hands, talking of the past and their times together, and watching their daughter and their dog play in the grass.

"I dreamed of this, too, Jimmy. Just like this. Please tell me this is real."

"My heart's about to come up through my throat, Crystal. I guess this is about as real as I have ever felt. I can't believe you are here, though. What are you doing here?"

"I live here now, Jimmy. Have ever since you last saw me. Soon as I started hitchhiking, Mrs. Tomlin—oh, that's my neighbor, actually, more like a mom to me than my own mother—picked me up and brought me here. Let me stay with her until I could get on my feet. Then we found out I was pregnant with Abby, and, well, I just stayed. You'll meet her, and, my oh my, will you have to do some explaining to her. I don't know if you have met any of the other women in this town, but they are one tough breed let me tell you."

Jimmy smiled and thought of Claudette.

"But you never know. She might take a shine to you. Or a baseball bat. And, now, I got me a little house, and I opened a hair salon. Make a pretty decent living at it, too."

Crystal looked back behind her at the townsfolk laughing, eating, and enjoying each other's company. She took Jimmy's arm and put it around her shoulder.

"I like it here, Jimmy. Demry is a nice place with bunches of nice folks. I feel safe here the way I used to feel safe with you. And what about you, Jimmy? What brings you through here on my lucky day wearing your Sunday best and all?"

"I broke down and was looking for a mechanic and ended up meeting this nice old lady. And she brought me here."

"Who'd you meet? If you don't mind me asking."

"Mrs. Claudette Burns."

Crystal started laughing. "Now there's a handful of a woman there. But I like her. She's like me. Speaks her mind she does."

"She sure does."

"I seen that guy Ringo and his boys messing around here this weekend. You ain't mixed up with them hooligans, are you?"

"No. I swear I broke down, and I mean it's a long story."

"I'm sure it is, Jimmy. Ain't nothing about you ever been a short story yet."

Crystal put her hand in his, and Jimmy closed his fingers around hers.

"I tell you what. Tell it to me over dinner tomorrow night at my house. I'm cooking."

Jimmy perked up on the bench, leaned over, and looked at her surprised. "You? You're cooking? You always hated to cook!"

"People change, Jimmy. Times are different now. It is either cook or starve. Didn't like my choices there, but cooking seemed the better option, don't you think?"

Jimmy took Crystal gently by the elbow and stood her up. Looking down into her sweet smiling face, he said, "I've got to tell you something really important. Give me just a minute to say it."

"If you gonna tell me you're dying of some incurable disease, you can't stop right there. I already thought you were dead once. I don't need to go breaking my heart again, especially now that you are a daddy."

Jimmy twisted the hairs of his beard in his hand. Crystal looked up at him. Her cheeks were flush, and she looked as though she was about to cry.

"I love your beard, Jimmy. It still looks good."

"Please stop for a minute. This is important."

He took both of her elbows in his hands, and she put her hands around his waist, hooking her thumbs in his belt. Jimmy licked his lips and cleared his throat.

"I'm sorry," he said. "I'm really, really sorry."

She put her head into his chest and snuggled up under his chin. "You should be sorry leaving me all alone in the middle of the desert like that. What were you thinking, Jimmy?"

"I think I felt that I was falling madly in love with you. And it scared the hell out of me."

"Oh, Jimmy, that's silly. Falling in love is one of the most natural things in the world. That and peeing, I guess."

Jimmy put his hand around her head and caressed her soft hair.

"And how about now, Jimmy? Still scared?"

"Terrified is more like it!"

"Terrified enough to run off again?"

"Not this time, baby. Not a chance."

"Oh, Jimmy, I missed you."

Crystal held her head against his chest and listened to his beating heart. I don't know why all of this is going on right now, but it's gotta mean something, doesn't it?"

The words came flowing right out of Jimmy's mouth, and, for the first time in his forty-three years, he uttered the words, "I guess what it means is I love you, Crystal. I've loved you since the first day I ever saw you."

She broke their embrace. There were tears flowing down her cheeks. She brushed them off with the back of her hands and looked at Jimmy. "I love you, too, Jimmy Star Two Fingers."

She went over to Abby and took her by the hand. "Come on, sweetie. Time to go home now. You've got school tomorrow. Say good-bye to Snoop."

Abby gave Snoop a pat on the head and grabbed Crystal's hand. Crystal was crying and trying to dry her cheeks with her palm.

"Mommy, are you crying?"

"Yes, pumpkin, Mommy's crying."

"Are you sad?"

"No, baby, Mommy is really, really happy."

"Then why are you crying?"

For the first time in her life, Crystal did not have a good answer for Abby.

"I don't know, baby. I don't know."

They began to walk away, and Crystal told Abby, "Go say good-bye, honey."

Abby turned and let go of her mother's hand. She ran over to Jimmy and hugged his leg. Looking up at him with her pigtails dangling behind, she said, "Bye-bye, Daddy."

Jimmy put his hand on top of her head. "Good-bye, honey."

Crystal blew Jimmy a kiss, and she and Abby walked away into the late Arizona afternoon under the cottonwoods and through the begonias.

Jimmy sat down on the bench, watching paper plates and napkins being blown by along the ground. He couldn't believe what had just happened. He put his hands together, looked to the sky, and said, "Thank you."

The sun sparkled around him like the gift he had just received. The emotions he felt were unlike anything he had ever experienced. That one touch, that one hug from his daughter around his leg, changed his life in an instant. His solitary toughness would be a thing of the past.

Nathan's voice drifted through the wind. *"Told you, Jimmy Star, anything's possible."* He sat silent for a long time, while Snoop licked the tears from his face.

Chapter 20

Claudette was sitting on her front porch when Jimmy returned. A cup of tea was by her side, and the Sunday paper was in her hand. She put it down as Jimmy approached.

"Oh, Mr. Two Fingers, come on up and join me."

She took a sip of tea and tipped the cup towards Jimmy as he sat down. "Would you like some?" she asked.

"I'd better hold off today, Claudette."

"You sure? No extras today, just the tea. I try and keep the Lord's Day as holy as possible, excepting when I don't!" Claudette giggled at herself.

Jimmy slipped into the chair next to Claudette, grimacing a bit from the stiffness in his knee. "Sounds like good judgment, Claudette"

"Looking out over the rim of her cup, Jimmy thought that her eyes looked tired. "Oh, you know me, sound as the day is long."

She laughed at herself again and put the cup down. "We missed you at the end of the picnic. I hope the food set you right. It certainly was a fine spread. One of the best so far!"

"Oh yes, the food was fine," Jimmy said.

"A rumor was spreading around the park that Mike Senderson had gotten his mitts on you and had taken you for a ride."

"No, nothing like that, Claudette, but you're not going to believe this."

Claudette perked up and scooted herself to the front of her chair. She put her elbows on her knees, and her chin in the palms of her hands. Jimmy was staring out over her shoulder at the lace curtains in her window.

Claudette impatiently waited for him to tell her. She noticed his faraway gaze and finally asked him, "Well, what is it?"

"Oh, oh, I'm sorry, Claudette, I am still just trying to wrap my head around it."

"Wrap your head around what, Mr. Two Fingers?"

"I saw Crystal this afternoon." It was a relief for Jimmy to say it. It made it all seem just that much more real and somehow okay.

Claudette's eyes got very big. She sat straight up, and she looked confused. "What? Crystal, your Crystal? Here in Demry? H-how, I mean, where?"

Jimmy shook his head and stared down at his boots, still not quite believing it himself. "Right there in the park, Claudette, over by the playground."

Claudette sat back in her chair and put her fingers to her mouth. "Oh my, my, my, my." What is she doing in Demry?"

"Seems she lives here—her and her daughter."

"Her daughter! Now, Mr. Two Fingers, you never told me she had a daughter."

"She didn't. At least when I was with her. Now, here's the kicker, she says the little girl is mine!"

Claudette got up out of her chair and rubbed her back. "Oh my, Mr. Two Fingers, now that is certainly a surprise. I think we are going to have to break the rules with the tea today."

She looked up and shook her hands as she walked across the porch. "Oh, Lord, forgive me, but we have issues today. If you'd like to sit in, you may be of service today. This man thought he just had car troubles. Oh, mercy, seems we are in a little deeper than that." She shook her head from side to side and went in the house.

Snoop jumped up on Jimmy's lap. "Well, Snoop, what do you think, boy? We've found ourselves in some funny situations in our life before. But this one is not so funny. Can't bully or buy ourselves out of this one."

Jimmy scratched Snoop behind the ears. "Sometimes I wish you could talk. I wonder what you would do if you were me."

Nathan's voice came to his head again. *"What would you do! Can't you see the signs, boy? Damn, she is one fine woman, and you been pining over her since she left. Now you sitting here, wondering what to do! Damn, boy, I've told you, indecision is a killer in this game. Now get off your ass and do what is right. I'm sure you know what is right, too. Make me proud of what I taught you for all those years. You thought it was just about the dope? What we talked about went way beyond hustling, Jimmy. I've told you what to do in situations you aren't sure of. Run if you have to, but working it out is always better than running. Now what you gonna do?"*

"What am I going to do?" Jimmy said.

Claudette came back out of the house with two glasses and a bottle of rum. She poured some in each glass and handed one to Jimmy. "What, no tea?" Jimmy asked.

"On days like these, Mr. Two Fingers..." She raised her glass to his, and they clinked. "...tea just gets in the way. Seems we are in a whole new ballgame now, aren't we?"

"Seems that way, Claudette."

"Oh, how excited you must be to have found her after all of this time! And a child to boot. The lord has certainly shined his light down on you today!"

"I'm not so sure I feel that way. I'm not really sure how I am supposed to feel."

Jimmy stared out over the soft desert sky. The sun was beginning to set. The crickets were beginning their chorus. The sound of them chirping soothed his nerves, which were jumping all over the place.

"Well, how did it feel to see her?"

"Oh, Claudette, my heart is still leaping around in my throat. I mean I can't believe this is all happening."

Claudette took a long, slow sip from her glass. "So what are you going to do now, Mr. Two Fingers?"

"Good question. I have been walking around for hours thinking about that, and my mind can't seem to concentrate long enough to make any kind of decision. I was surprised as all get out to see her. My heart started pounding like a teenager on a Friday night. It all just happened so fast. And then to find out I might be that little girl's father...well, it's just a little too hard for me to take it all in right now."

"Sounds like love to me! But funny thing about decisions, though, is they tend to get made up when they want to, not when you want them to."

"Is that so?"

"Yep, that's so."

"What do you mean, Claudette?"

Claudette put down her glass and looked out at the houses up and down her street. "Take the case of my husband passing. He didn't just up and decide to die. That decision came all on its own."

"What do you think I should do?"

"Do? If I was you, I'd go rustle me up a big bunch of flowers and hightail on over to her place and ask her to marry me! But I'm just romantic like that, and really haven't known you long enough to be running my decisions for you. But from what you were telling me last night, you'd do anything to be back in her arms again."

Claudette took another sip of rum and continued. "Seems the Lord put her right down in your lap. If that ain't telling you something, then you need to go fill that hole in your head and shut it for good."

Jimmy felt the tension, the anxiety, and the loneliness that had crept in and stayed in his heart for many years deeply in his chest. And it made him sad. He took a big swallow of rum. It made him wince as it went down his throat.

"What's the worst thing that could happen, Mr. Two Fingers?"

Jimmy got up and went over to the railing of the porch and looked over the horizon. The first stars were beginning to appear. The hub-bub, the noise and chatter of the day in his mind, began to ease a bit.

"There is no worst thing, Claudette. I am very excited that I got to see Crystal. It's just that I never expected it to happen the way that it did."

"How did you expect it to happen, Mr. Two Fingers?"

Jimmy closed his eyes and rubbed his temples with his forefingers and thumb. "I don't know. I guess I thought, maybe, I would run into her at a restaurant waiting tables or at a store somewhere. She would get in the van, and we'd ride off into the sunset. All good like that in the storybooks. I never expected it to be here this weekend. And for her to be a mother of a beautiful young girl to boot..."

"Life's not a storybook, Jimmy. I can see it in your face that something's not sitting right, Mr. Two Fingers. What is it?"

Jimmy hesitated and fidgeted, looking for the words he wanted to use. "No offense, Claudette, Demry is a nice town and all, but I'm used to being on the road. And the road is no place to be raising a child."

"So what is it you do out there on the road, Mr. Two Fingers?"

"Well, let's just say I'm a lot more like those bikers than the townsfolk around here."

Claudette poured more rum into her glass and let it swirl around in the ice before taking a sip. "Seems to me you're going about putting blocks in the way of your happiness that just don't need to be there. On one hand, you've been telling me you've been looking for this woman for years, and then the Lord comes and plunks her down right in front of you. And now you're telling me this ain't your kind of town. What's one got to do with the other? You are getting that cart way out in front of you. And you're about to roll it all the way down the hill, and let it get away from you without even peeking inside to see what's in there!" Claudette took another sip and asked, "How did you feel when you saw her in the park?"

"I felt like my prayers had been answered, and my heart had opened up."

"And now how do you feel?"

Jimmy looked down at his boots and stared at them. He felt like the child he used to be when he was left alone. He didn't know how to make his emotions work for him, and he would just clam up. "Confused."

"Jimmy, I have got to let you in on a little thing that most folks already know."

Jimmy lifted his head and looked towards Claudette. A streak of hair had come out from where it was tied and hung across his face. He was surprised but also felt a sense of kinship when she called him Jimmy.

"Jimmy, come sit." Jimmy sat back down, and Claudette pulled her chair up so that she was right in front of him. She reached for his hands, and he put his hands in hers.

Her skin felt warm and soft against his rough skin. His heart began to beat faster, and he felt a tear behind his eye. When she closed her hands around his, the tear fell out and ran down his cheek. He didn't know why he was crying, but it felt good to feel his heart begin to open up again. As painful as it was to see his heart being torn again, he knew that seeing Crystal could only mean one thing, that he still had a chance at love. He also realized that you don't have to know someone for a lifetime for them to be a kind and decent human being towards you.

Claudette waited patiently for Jimmy to look up. "Jimmy, what you felt in the park was real. As real as you and I sitting here. What is not real is the fear and the excuses for not allowing yourself the happiness that you deserve. That's just your head talking. Seems like it may have been talking you out of things most of the time. It happens, Jimmy. It happens to all of us. You just have to recognize it for what it is, and then tell it to shut the hell up!"

"I've just never been in a situation like this before, and I don't want to blow it again."

"Well, then, don't blow it, but at least give yourself the chance. Let her know how you feel. Men always think it's a crime to be afraid and confused. She will understand your fears, Jimmy. If she does love you, she will understand."

"No one has ever talked to me like this before, Claudette. I'm not sure what to say."

"You don't have to say anything, Jimmy. You're going to see her again, right?"

"Yes, we are having dinner tomorrow."

"Good, just make sure you tell her how you feel, how you really feel. Don't hold back. There is something in the air that hangs around you, Jimmy. Something your soul has been feeling for, and for what I'm guessing, has been there a very long time. Probably longer than you know. And you can't let it die out on this porch without tending to it."

Jimmy had hung his head again, listening to Claudette's words, and deep inside, he knew they were true. Claudette took one of her hands and put it on the side of his face. Jimmy looked up and into her eyes.

"Like I said, I'm a romantic. And I would give anything, I mean anything, to have a love like that in my life again. Now, here's the secret no one has let you in on."

"What's that, Claudette?"

"Jimmy, love is the only thing that matters."

Chapter 21

S leep came slowly for Jimmy. Like a faraway freight train, its whistle was teasing an arrival that didn't come. Jimmy stared at the ceiling of his van. It was dull and grey. Snoop was making little squeaks as he slept in the front seat. He would usually cuddle up close to Jimmy at night. But even he was not privy to Jimmy's heart, and the loneliness that scared him.

The thoughts meandered through his mind. *What am I so afraid of? Is this what I really wanted all along? Or am I just fooling myself into believing I could have the love I thought I wanted.*

Jimmy sat up and got his bag of weed from the console. He wrapped a neat little joint and licked the paper shut. He let it dry, and he unrolled the vent in the roof. The spark of the lighter lit the van in glowing light that did not quite reach the corners. He lit a small candle on the shelf and watched the flame flicker.

The sweet aroma of the *indica* he smoked filled the van, and a small smokestack arose to the ceiling and crept its way out into the night. Jimmy smoked the whole joint, taking several big hits at a time, then letting it go out until he was ready again. The ritual was one that he had repeated almost every night that he could remember.

His mind had shifted gears and took him back to the day he had last seen Crystal before she abruptly left the van, and his life. It was another hot scorching day in Arizona, and they were heading back down south to pick up a load for clients. The easiness of the road was something that Jimmy relished, and this day started out no differently. For a while at least.

The morning ninety-degree temperatures gave way to the hundreds around noon, and even having the windows down was no respite from the relentless swelter. The invisible waves of heat were bouncing up off the blacktop, and the dust clung low to the ground.

"Jimmy, can we go to California soon?" Crystal asked.

Jimmy thought about his schedule and how much money he wanted to make over the next few months. California was not in his plans, and he gave her a flat, "No we can't."

"Why not Jimmy, I'm getting tired of looking at cactus all of the time. We need some excitement."

The heat and Crystal's voice were irritating Jimmy. This was the busy time of year for him. The harvests were rotating, and he planned to get on as much of the action as he could. The smell of green money and weed were on the forefront of his mind. Not California.

"Crystal, we've been through this before, honey. We've got to make hay while the sun is shining." Jimmy looked up through the tinted strip that ran across the top of the windshield. The bugs and grime from the road had coated the windshield and made him squint.

"And if you look up there, the sun is shining."

Crystal lit up one of her long cigarettes and blew smoke rings towards the windshield. Jimmy looked at Crystal until she looked back at him. Then he looked at her hand holding the cigarette and nodded. "That's why the windshield is always glaring."

Crystal slumped on the seat and took another long drag. "What the hell are you talking about, Jimmy?"

"It's the cigarette smoke that makes these windows so foggy and hard to see."

"That's crazy, Jimmy. Look at all them damn bugs collecting out there." Crystal pointed with the hand she held the cigarette with and flicked the ash on the dash. "That's why you can't see out the damn window."

Jimmy turned on the air conditioner, and a puff of dust preceded the hot air that blew out.

"You know, that damn thing ain't working so well. I told you, you should go get it fixed last time we were in Flagstaff. But no, Mister Fixit said he could do it himself."

Jimmy's neck began to sweat, and the stale smell of tobacco was churning his stomach. "Put that thing out, would you? It's making me sick."

Crystal scrunched one side of her nose and raised her eyebrow. "What the hell are you talking about, Jimmy? After two years, they are just now making you feel sick."

Crystal took another long drag and blew it out the window. She watched the smoke quickly escape and said under her breath, "I ain't putting out my cigarette."

"What did you say?" Jimmy barked.

"I ain't said nothing to you, Jimmy. Mind your own damn business!"

Jimmy pulled his glasses from his eyes and lifted them onto the top of his head. He looked at Crystal and scowled. "Anything that happens in my van is my business. Got it!"

"Oh, I got it all right! Seems you are forgetting that I been in this damn van for two goddamn years with you, and now you're gonna pull this 'my fucking van' thing!" Crystal lifted one of her long legs up off the floor and kicked at the glove compartment with her heel. It flew open, and the contents that were stuffed in there spilled out onto the floor and onto Snoop, who was lying below Crystal's legs.

Snoop scurried from underneath the pile of candy wrappers, gum spray, napkins, hairbrushes, and everything else that came spilling out. He startled Jimmy when he jumped into his lap. Jimmy looked down at the floor, and then to Snoop, and momentarily took his eyes off the road. A loud pull from the air horn of the diesel semitruck barely seventy-five yards away got his attention, as they were both barreling towards each other.

"Jimmy, look out!" Crystal shrieked.

Jimmy had drifted over the yellow line and into the opposite lane, where the bright black semi was racing towards them. Jimmy turned the wheel quickly with both hands to the right and out of the oncoming traffic. Then he made a quick short pull to the left to keep from fishtailing out of control.

The trucker laid on his horn until they passed each other and were out of harm's way. The drinks that were in the console spilled all over the papers and everything else that had come out of the glove compartment.

"Fuck! That was close, Jimmy. Pay goddamn attention to the road, would you!" Crystal's hands were shaking, and her face had gone flush. "You almost got us killed there!"

Jimmy's hands were also shaking. Snoop, who also became upset, jumped in the back of the van and curled into a tight little ball. His tail was tucked and only his head was poking out, revealing his shaken and scared eyes.

Jimmy found a small dirt pull off and stopped the van. Crystal was busy picking up the papers from the floor and shaking the sticky soda from them. Jimmy quickly dragged his hands through his hair, knocking his glasses off his head and down behind the seat. "Goddamn it!" he yelled.

"Yelling ain't helping none here, Jimmy!"

The agitation they were both feeling from being cooped up in the van for the last few days in the hot Arizona sun had boiled over into a full-blown argument, with neither of them willing to give way to the other. The back and forth had reached a fever pitch that didn't want to end.

"All I wanted to do was go to the fucking beach for a few days, but no, you're shit is way more important than anybody else! I've had it with this shit!"

Crystal crawled over the seat and quickly gathered her few belongings, including Bessie, and threw them in her pack. She crawled back over the seat and reached for the door handle.

"Where the hell do you think you're going?"

"Who knows? Maybe California, I don't know. But I'm sure as hell getting away from you." Crystal's cheeks had turned bright red, and her hair was falling down into her face, the ends popping up and down near her mouth as she yelled. "I can't believe you would treat me like this, Jimmy. After all the times you told me you loved me, you go ahead and start acting like this. Typical fucking man. All good until a woman speaks her own mind. Then you go all Neanderthal on me. I'm fucking out of here."

Her words hit Jimmy in a hollow place that he had long forgotten. The place of fear, resentment, and disillusion had opened in a heartbeat, and he was left with nothing to say. He stared at the steering wheel, and, in an instant, all the loneliness he had ever felt in his life rushed back in and filled the hollow hole. It was a place it knew well, and it had returned, blanking out any sense or reason he had come to have.

Crystal stared Jimmy down, waiting for him to say something. He just looked straight ahead and spit on the floor.

That was all she could take. Tears flowed from her eyes, and she opened the door and stepped out of the van. She looked back in at him one more time and said, "I love you, Jimmy Star Two Fingers. But this time, you pushed my nerves too far."

Jimmy never looked up at her as he said, "Well, darling, adi-fuckin'-os to you, too. Don't let the door hit you on your way down the road!"

That cold feeling of all of his wrongs felt good in a way that he had forgotten. He jammed the van into gear, and he sped off.

Chapter 22

Jimmy closed the vent, and blew out the candle. Snoop crawled in the back, curled himself into a ball, and fell asleep by Jimmy's side

Still unable to sleep himself, he let the scenes of the fight pass away from his memory and thought back to happier times he had had with Crystal. And there had been many. All Crystal ever really had to do to perk Jimmy up was to smile at him. She would put her fingers near his temple and twirl his hair while saying his name. "Jimmy, Jimmy!"

It was a game they would play. She would twirl his hair and blow her soft warm breath into his ear. He would try not to look at her for as long as he could take. But in the end, she always won. He would eventually give in and look at her. And her bright wide smile would be looking back at him. This was as in love as he had ever felt.

So why am I so afraid now? She says she forgives me and wants me to see her tomorrow. And her little girl, our little girl is the sweetest little thing. No reason for me to deny she is my daughter. Crystal never lied to me. She can't keep anything in long enough to conjure up a lie. Her head and mouth are way too quick for that.

But he was afraid. Afraid he would leave himself wide open to his heart again. He thought he knew better, and everything Claudette had said on the porch made perfect sense to him. However, his mind turned and thought of every scenario that could make things turn out unfavorable.

But deep inside, when he closed his eyes and thought back to the park when Crystal had taken her hat off, and he saw and smelled her hair, he knew that he was still in love with her. And when young Abby had called him Daddy, he had turned into a puddle.

I know I will see her again, and I will feel like I did then. But what if I don't? What if my longing was just because she was my lover, and I just missed her?

Nathan's voice joined the party of conflicting thoughts that ran through Jimmy's mind.

"Jimmy, you need to settle them old fears down now and get about your business. And your present business is following your heart and see where it leads you to. Don't you go fretting now about everything that can go wrong. That's just foolish. You done learned to make the best of bad deals now, haven't you?"

Jimmy silently answered himself, *Yes.*

"And most of the time, you come out on the right side of the stick, too. This ain't no different; it's just another part of life that you ain't been that practiced in. Listen, when I took you up off the street and turned you into a businessman, you didn't barely no anything about hustling or money or anything. But I liked you. You had spunk behind that hard-ass head of yours."

Jimmy thought of the day he had met Nathan. He did take him from a two-bit street punk into a man who was respected, feared, and sought out for his skills, his demeanor, and his guts.

Nathan was one of the only people who had taken a genuine interest in Jimmy and guided him into becoming a man. A spark lit in Jimmy's head, His chest shuddered, making Snoop jump up.

He had known but never let himself admit that he feelings he had for Nathan went far beyond respect. He had genuine love for this man. Jimmy held onto this feeling right up until the moment he fell asleep.

Chapter 23

Jimmy awoke and went about his morning routine. He had heard Claudette leave earlier to attend Rita Simpson's funeral. His mind and heart were still spinning their dance inside of him. He tried to put it aside for now and get down to business. He needed to get his van fixed, and he still had twenty pounds of pot to deliver. That and he would be seeing Crystal later for dinner.

Suddenly, his life seemed to be very busy. But a breakdown will do that to you. And a break up. And a reconciliation, if you can call it that. Despite his best efforts, the chatter in his mind continued.

Chapter 24

"I'll tell you what...what did you say your name was again?"

"Oh, just call me Jimmy."

"Well, Jimmy, if you want to get your van fixed, it's gonna take me a few days to get to it."

Gus Winkler motioned with his weathered hands to the other vehicles lined up outside of his shop, waiting their turn to be repaired, revamped, or retired.

"You could drive down to Tucson, and maybe get it in a little quicker. But it's about eighty miles from here, and I don't even need to hoist her up on the jack to tell you it's your water pump that needs replacing. The way it's leaking, it'd be touch and go for you in this heat."

Gus used the sleeve of his oil-stained grey coveralls and wiped the beads of sweat from his forehead. His bright green eyes blazed underneath his tired eyelids and wrinkled forehead. The ball cap he wore had a picture of a truck that was so faded Jimmy could barely make it out.

"The leak is just gonna get worse. You can leave it here, if you want, and check back, uh, maybe tomorrow afternoon, if'n I could get the parts up here. Can't say for sure."

Gus gave Jimmy a look up and down. Noticing his wrinkled shirt, Gus asked, "You living here or just passing through."

"Just passing through for now, Gus. Me and Snoop here." Jimmy motioned with his thumb to the open driver's window in the van. Gus walked over, and Snoop popped his head out and eagerly wagged his tail.

"Oh, little fella, aren't you just full of spunk today!" Gus reached in the pants pocket of his coveralls and produced a small dog biscuit. He turned to Jimmy. "Okay if I give him this?"

"Sure, he is gonna get fat before leaving this town."

"There you go, little fella." Gus watched as Snoop took the biscuit and scurried to the floor with it.

Gus pulled a wooden pipe out of his pocket and tapped the ashes out into his calloused hand. "I'd send you down to Billy Simpsons, but his wife passed and today is the funeral."

"Yeah, I heard that."

"Well, bad news does travel fast in a small town. Not like there is anywhere else for it to go, though. Poor, Rita, she's been sick for some time. Shame to see her like that. She was so full of life and energy before she got sick, and now, well, you know. Poor, Billy, he's putting up a good front, but I know he's just breaking inside."

"What man wouldn't be?" Jimmy added.

"Heh, you'd be surprised at how spiteful some men can be to their wives." Gus shook his head back and forth. He looked inside the van. "Looks like you're pretty self-sufficient in this van. There's a campground down the road a few miles. Real nice place to stay. I'll order the pump. I can send word down there when it comes in. Only take me a few hours to put it in."

The oil stains on Gus's shirt told their own story, and Jimmy knew his van be in good hands with him.

"Looks like were spending the night in Demry, Snoop."

"Good, good," Gus said as he reached his fingers into a leather pouch and filled his pipe with tobacco.

"Like I say, though, might take a day or two for me to get the part. Don't work on too many Astros. Usually, don't need to. Good vehicles. Now, if it was one of these pieces of shit back here"—Gus pointed behind him with his thumb to a bright yellow minivan.

"Damn things break down all of the time! And after about four years, the dealers won't touch them without charging you two arms and then some. They knew they were junk when they were selling them in the first place."

Gus put his pipe to his mouth and struck a stick match on the garage wall. He watched the flame grow and put it to the bowl. His cheeks sank in as he puffed the tobacco to life. A sweet smell arose from the pipe. Jimmy thought to himself, *If somebody could just make pot that smelled like that, we'd be in big-time money.*

"Tried to tell people to stay away from them in the first place, but nobody listens to old people anymore."

Gus swatted at the gnats that began to peck at the sweat just below his collar. "But, heck, what do I know? I just been turning wrenches for almost fifty years. Young folks just don't listen to their elders like they used to. Even my son. Heck, things used to run a lot smoother around here when he was here."

He looked towards the ground and kicked at the heat that was beginning to rise off the blacktop. "But he decided that Demry was not the place for him. He was gonna see the world."

Jimmy thought to himself that if he grew up here, he would have probably been itching to get out of here also.

"Funny thing is, though, he only made it as far as Tucson. Of all things, his car broke down." Gus looked at his knuckles, then back at Jimmy. "He took a job there and stayed on. Guess that was, oh, four years ago now. I don't blame him, though. I guess he never saw a chance of anything, except for ending up like his old man, if he stayed around here."

Gus kicked at the loose gravel again. "I sure do miss him, though."

The old mechanic dropped his head again. He put his pipe back in his pocket, pulled out an oily rag, and dropped his hands into it. Wiping the ash and what grease he could, he shook his head and said to Jimmy, "Excuse me, I need a moment."

"Of course." Jimmy watched Gus walk back into the garage and out of his sight.

Damn, did my old man ever think that way about me? he thought to himself. He looked down at Snoop. "Probably not, Snoop," he said out loud.

Jimmy walked into the garage. He liked the way it smelled. There was always something he liked about the smell, feel, and look of a garage that held his fascination ever since he was a boy. He looked around the garage. Attached, hanging, sitting, or leaning on the various shelves, cabinets, and tables were oil cans, antifreeze, spark plugs, wires, grinders, tools, and all sorts of odd nuts and bolts.

Hanging over the table that had a vise grip over an old alternator was Jimmy's favorite thing about garages. No matter where in the world you were, this was the one thing that all garages had in common—the obligatory calendar with a bikini-clad long-legged woman leaning over the hood of a hot rod! Jimmy leaned in for a closer look. Its page was still set on February.

Gus came back and stopped next to Jimmy. "Yeah, she's my favorite." He laughed. "You got any kids?" he asked Jimmy.

"N-no, I mean yes. Yes, I have a daughter."

Gus looked at him from the corner of his eyes as he was wiping the grime from the outside of the alternator. "You don't sound so sure.

"Sorry, but, yes, I do have a daughter." His heart opened when he said this, and he felt a strange sense of pride creep up from somewhere hidden long ago.

"Well, if you want some advice from an old man, spend as much time with her as you can. Once they grow up and go out on their own, you never know where they are gonna end up."

"Thanks. I'll remember that, Gus."

"You do that. Of course, it won't make the heartache any better if they do go away. But at least you'll see it coming.

Jimmy never in his dreams believed he would be listening intently to advice about what to do with children. He looked back at the calendar, and a shiver ran down his back.

"Anyway, your van should be all right for a few miles at least, if you need to go somewhere. Or you can just leave it here. I just got off the phone with the parts department. Your water pump should be here by tomorrow afternoon. Have you all fixed up by Wednesday at the latest."

"That'd be great, Gus. I'll check in with you tomorrow."

Jimmy was walking out of the garage when Gus called from behind him. "That campground is about five miles from here, if you're looking for a nice place to stay. Looks like your all set up for sleeping in your van. Nice woman runs the place, too. Your van should make it back and forth from there at least."

"Thanks. I think I will head down there. See you tomorrow, Gus."

Chapter 25

The road to the campground wound through a small canyon lined with Sycamore trees, large oaks, and cottonwoods. The green lushness of it all made it feel much cooler than it really was. The Arizona sun was heating the day and making him uncomfortable. He knew that he should not use his air conditioner, with his van being in the state it was in.

Jimmy's thoughts turned to Crystal and Abby. Confusion about what to do was forefront on his mind. He looked into his rearview mirror. When he saw nobody behind him, he pulled a joint out from his ashtray and lit it up. He took a long hit and held the ember to his nose, inhaling the sweet aroma until his lungs were filled. He slowly let it out, and he felt his mind ease from its tension.

Another hit like the last one was all he would need for now. He liked to be stoned when driving, but found he functioned better with strangers when he was straight. And who knows what "the nice woman" who ran the campground would be like.

The smell of antifreeze was still strong, and Jimmy kept a close eye on the temperature gauge the rest of the way down the lush green canyon.

"Well, Snoop, we're off to a campground."

Snoop jumped into Jimmy's lap and licked at his neck until Jimmy started laughing.

They pulled into the Double D campground. The place looked deserted. They pulled up to a wooden cabin that had a sign under the yellow awning that said, "Office."

The door opened, and a round woman much too large for the size of her feet came bounding out, eagerly waving her hand at him. She was wearing a bright white dress with black polka dots on it. The dress was wrapped so tightly around her that it looked like she could fall out of it at any second. Her hair was jet-black and pushed up high on top of her head. Bright red lipstick graced her small lips, and her cheeks were blushed.

Jimmy watched amusedly as she walked around the front of the van and stuck her hand in the driver's window. Jimmy took it in his, and they shook. "You must be Jimmy!"

"Am I famous around here already? How'd you know my name?"

The woman batted her overly made up eyes, and, in a squeaky voice that sounded too small for her body, said, "Well, you might be famous. I mean, for around here, you're already famous for having that run in with that jerk Mike Senderson,

She snooped around the front of the van with her eyes and lifted her nose to the air. "Anyway, that's not how I know your name. No, not that at all. I just got off the phone with Gus. Told me you might be heading my way. I'd sure be glad to have you. Everyone else cleared out this morning now that Demry days is over. Plenty of room for you and your little dog there."

She gave a small wave at Snoop, who was sitting up in the passenger seat, licking his paws and not paying attention to anything going on around him. Then her mouth opened as wide as her eyes did, showing two rows of perfectly straight white teeth. Her hand went to her mouth, and a big smile crossed her face.

She pointed at Jimmy, and then to Snoop. "I knew it! I knew it! You're that man with the famous dog that does all the tricks at the circus and carnivals, aren't you? She jumped up and down in place, her body threatening to burst loose from her dress. She clapped her hands together.

"I knew someone famous was gonna come to Doris D's campground someday. I just knew it!"

Jimmy looked at her enthusiasm and was glad he was stoned for this one. "Well, I hate to burst your bubble on you, darling, especially seeing as how nice you got all dressed up for me. But you got the wrong guy." He looked at Snoop, who was still licking away, and told her, "Ain't nothing famous about us two. And, as much as I like to think that my dog is almost as handsome as I am, ol' Snoop here ain't much for doing tricks. Are you, Snoop?"

Doris slumped and snapped her finger, making a sharp pop. "Shoot, I thought today would be that day." Her frown quickly turned to a smile. She pushed her thumb back towards the sign hanging over a small rusty pole that had floodlights minus any bulbs living in their sockets, and proudly proclaimed, "I'm Doris D! And famous or not, I'm still glad to have you here!"

Jimmy couldn't help himself seeing how she was dressed. "I hope you didn't get all dressed up for someone famous, and then I let you down now, sugar."

Doris looked down at her dress and gently wiped some dust off the material just above her shoulder. "No, no, tonight's bingo night, and you never know who is going to come to bingo night, especially right after Demry days. No one wants this party to end."

"In case you didn't notice, Doris D, it ain't even lunch time yet."

"I know, but I don't like to wait to get dressed up. I missed the dance the other night, seeing I was so busy here. And a girl can get dressed up nice and look pretty if she wants to, right?"

"You are right there, darling, and if'n I do say so myself, you look very nice in that dress."

"Well, thank you. That's very nice of you to say, Mr....uh.

"Oh, call me Jimmy, and, uh, this is Snoop, the not-so-wonder dog. But he is a good buddy of mine, and should not cause any of your other guests any trouble."

Doris looked around the campground. "You got the place to yourself so far today, Mr. Jimmy. Why don't you try one of those spots back there in those trees? You'll get a little more shade in there. Shower's around the back of the office here. If you need anything else, just let me know. I'll be here until about four."

"Well, thank you, Doris. I may be here a few days."

"Yeah, that's what Gus said. If you want, you could come on into town and play bingo later."

Jimmy's addled mind considered the idea for just a second, and he laughed. "I don't think I could keep up with the bingo sharks around here, Doris. You gals would probably eat me alive at the bingo table!"

"Oh, we're not so bad. I mean, except for a few of the women that come in that are just strictly business. Don't even barely lift their heads up from the table. You know the type."

"I'm afraid I don't, Doris."

"That's okay. You really don't need to. They are no fun anyway. I just like to go for fun and companionship. Gets lonely out here by myself. Who knows? Maybe one day, I might meet my future husband there." Doris bit her lower lip and scanned her eyes back and forth across the ground. "Or somewhere."

Jimmy took this as an invitation of sorts, and thought it would be best to get on his way before the conversation led him to somewhere he didn't want to go. He knew darn well that when he was stoned, he could flirt with the best of them. But now was not the time or place to consider such an outing. *No, not today, Jimmy boy,* he thought to himself. *Not tonight. You have a date with the woman you've been looking for for a very long time.*

"Well, Doris, I do appreciate your hospitality." Jimmy put the van in gear, and, just before stepping on the gas pedal, he stuck his head out the window and said, "Best of luck to you out there tonight, Doris. You never know when that right person is gonna show up. But when they do, you will know."

Jimmy felt funny that it was his turn to pass on sagely advice on a subject that he did know something about.

Chapter 26

After a shower, Jimmy laid out a comfortable and clean set of clothes to wear to Crystal's tonight. She had given him directions and asked him to come over at seven. His hands began to sweat just thinking about seeing her again.

"Now, Snoop, you stay off of these clothes now. We need to be presentable when we arrive tonight."

Snoop's ears perked up, as if he knew what he had said, and he jumped over the backseat of the van and inspected Jimmy's outfit with his nose.

"I told you, Snoop, stay away from these now." Jimmy laughed at Snoop as he nosed his way around the outside of his clean shirt and pants.

The campground bordered a state park, but it was far from the entrance. A stream bed trickled by, still flowing from the previous monsoon season's rain. The white bark of the sycamore shone brightly in the midafternoon sun.

The heat of the day was upon them. He was thankful to be near water and in the shade. While not the full force of summertime, it was still very hot in this part of the world.

His life of travel had brought him all around the United States, but it was the Southwestern region that he fell in love with the first time he drove through. And it was the little hamlets, valleys, arroyos, and out-of-the-way places like this one that kept him here. Despite the few months of intense heat, he preferred it to other well-known and more profitable routes.

Jimmy pulled a chair out of the van and set it out close to the creek. As he sat, he thought back to the people he had met in the last few days, and the circumstances that surrounded the situations that he had come across. He felt so thankful for each one of them. For if there was any other turn of events, he may not have ran into Crystal and Abby.

"I might have just drove on past there and never seen her again, Snoop. That would've sucked!" Jimmy was still very stoned, and, as he talked to Snoop. He found it amusing that it was with this little dog that he had his deepest and longest lasting relationship. "Yep, you and me, Snoop, we go back a ways now." Snoop lay on a cool patch of grass. His ears perked up at any time Jimmy would mention his name.

"But now, we got this, Snoop. I can't believe that I have a daughter. It hasn't even sunk in yet. What am I gonna do with a daughter? I don't know anything about being a dad. But then again, neither did my dad, or my mom, for that fact."

He picked up a small stone from beside his chair and tossed it into a small pool in the creek. The water rippled back and forth against itself before becoming calm again. A few stones later, Jimmy found himself beginning to doze off, but would quickly snap his head back up when his chin would touch his chest. After a few more head bobbles, he let it stay where it was, and he drifted into sleep.

Chapter 27

A low rumble filled his ears as he dreamed of a day on a beach. He and two people he did not know were trying to lift a beach ball out of the water. The rumble was coming from beyond the sand dunes.

As it got closer, a light began to creep in behind his eyes, and he could hear himself snoring. The light became brighter, and he put his hands to his eyes and realized that the rumbling noise was him snoring.

But, as he took a deep breath and began to rub his eyes, the rumbling was indeed getting louder, and it was, in fact, getting closer each second. He shook his head, trying to clear the fog of sleep from his brain.

He looked down and saw Snoop still lying there with his eyes open and his head on the ground. Then the sound became apparent. He rubbed his eyes and listened to the unmistakable sound of a Harley Davidson engine that pulled up in front of his van. A few loud revs filled the air around him. Then the engine was silenced.

Jimmy stretched his arms and back. Raising his arms to the sky, he got up out of his chair. Snoop jolted up out of his grassy bed and began to bark. Without turning to look yet, Jimmy figured that the rider could only be one person. And it was. Ringo James's shadow preceded him as he came around to the back of the van.

"What's up, Jimmy Star Two Fingers?"

Just barely awake, Jimmy pulled the hair back away from his eyes, and he held it on top of his head, his eyes scouring the ground for his hair tie.

"Get that mop cut, and you don't have to worry about shit like that!" Ringo's heavy voice boomed.

Snoop raced around Ringo, barking but staying well away from Ringo's long legs.

"Yeah, I know, but then I run the risk like you of getting a sunburn on the top of my head. No thanks. I'll keep my hair."

Jimmy gave up looking for his hair tie and walked over to Ringo, putting out his hand as he did. "Knock it off, Snoop! It's all right."

"Quite the little yapper you got there, Jimmy." Ringo obliged Jimmy, and they shook hands.

Jimmy was still a little disoriented by being woken, and he shook his head and put his finger in both ears and scratched. "What's my pleasure all about this time, Ringo?" Jimmy took a sip of water from his cup, and then asked, "And how did you find me here, anyway?"

"Small town, Jimmy. Not too hard to find someone when you're looking for them."

Jimmy pulled another folding chair from the back of the van and set it across from his. "Hope this holds you up. Come on, let's sit down. I just woke up."

"Yeah, it looks like it."

Ringo was back in his jeans, leathers, and vest today. He unfolded the canvas chair and sat down across from Jimmy, squeezing himself in between the two armrests.

"So, why you looking, anyway?"

"Figured we had some hatchets to bury, and I'm heading out of town tonight. Thought I'd stop by and say good-bye."

"That's mighty right of you. How come I don't believe you?"

"Good intuition there, Jimmy."

Jimmy looked crossways at Ringo. He knew this was not a courtesy visit, or a man with his past regrets trying to come clean. No, Ringo was too proud, mean, and stubborn for such nonsense. But he was here.

"Okay, what gives, Ringo?"

"Your friend there from the park, what's her name?"

Jimmy's mind immediately went to Crystal. How would he have found out so quickly? It was just late yesterday, small town and all. But this didn't add up for Jimmy.

"What friend would that be, Ringo?"

"The one you had lunch with when I stomped on that loud mouth."

"You mean, Claudette."

"Yeah, yeah, I guess that is her name."

"What about her? Is she all right?" Jimmy's nerve turned from confused to worried.

"Not exactly, Jimmy."

Jimmy scooched to the front of his chair and leaned towards Ringo. "What happened, Ringo?"

"You know we had the funeral today."

"Yeah, I heard about that."

"Well, after the funeral, we all went back to my uncle's house." Ringo swatted at the flies that had congregated around his arms and neck. "We were all having lunch, and she just sort of passed out and hit her head on the sidewalk."

"Heart attack?" Jimmy asked.

"Don't know, Jimmy. The paramedics came, and she was conscious when they took her away. Sent everybody through the ringer it did."

Jimmy twisted his beard in his fingers, leaving his thoughts of Crystal and Abby behind for a moment.

"Heard all kinds of stories about her after that, though. Seems she's made quite a name for herself as being a firecracker and putting people in their place for generations now."

"Yep, that sounds like her."

"Anybody say if she would be all right?"

"Nobody seemed to know, but they were gonna bring her to the hospital and do some tests I guess."

Jimmy turned and looked down at Snoop. His heart felt heavy. *How could the course of a weekend turn my feelings into feelings?* he quickly thought. *It's not like I never had any, but now I've got them coming out of the woodwork.*

"Damn, I guess I better get into town and go see her."

"Better pick a number. Half the people at my uncle's were talking about going to see her."

"I bet."

Ringo looked up at the sturdy branches of the sycamore tree. Then he looked past the creek, and up the canyon wall. "Nice place you got here, Jimmy. You staying a while?"

"Don't know yet. I've got a few things to work out."

"You working or just passing through?"

Jimmy looked up at Ringo and gave a little smile.

"Yeah, thought so. Who you working with these days?"

Jimmy sat silent for a moment, contemplating whether it mattered if he told Ringo who he was partnered up with in his latest endeavors. He decided it didn't matter.

"Oh, you know."

Ringo let out a strong laugh that made his belly move up and down under his thick black leather jacket. "You know, that's another thing I've always liked about you, Jimmy. Always did keep your damn mouth shut!"

"Comes with the territory, Ringo. You know that."

"Yeah, you and me know that. But a lot of these new fucking yahoos we got working out there these days don't seem to mind throwing people's names around, especially when they get popped. Pisses me right the fuck off that the honor and integrity that comes with the game is being shut aside out of stupidity, ego, and lack of respect!"

Jimmy rocked his shoulders back and forth while he listened to Ringo telling a few tales of his recent wanderings to Mexico and Southern California. He thought of all the times he had crossed the border before things really clamped down and put a crimp in the marijuana trade. The crimp was short lived, though, as dealers and buyers were always going to find a way to make a deal and get the product to where the consumers would purchase it.

Tunnels were built. Airplanes and small boats were used much more these days. Secret compartments were being built into vehicles, making it much more difficult for authorities to find and seize contraband. Jimmy would occasionally read in a newspaper about large busts, and politicians ranting about how they were going to be the ones to shut down the drug trade. They knew, as well as the participants in the industry, that this would never happen. Truth of the matter is—and Jimmy always knew this—that if someone was willing to pay good money for a commodity, there would always be someone there to sell it to them. Simple mathematics and predictable human behavior had always fetched a good price on the open market. The same market that had made Jimmy and Ringo money for most of their lives.

With the sleep leaving his eyes and mind, Jimmy's thoughts awoke to Crystal and Abby. While he was not willing to let Ringo in on his business dealings, he was curious to find out what his take on his current situation would be.

"Before you go, Ringo, you mind if I ask you something?"

"Who said I was going anywhere, Jimmy? I kind of like this quiet little spot you got here. Fact, I might have to go find me a little yapping dog and become your neighbor."

Jimmy had always appreciated Ringo's wit and humor, but knew he never stuck round too long.

"Oh, I think this might be a little too quiet for your likes, Ringo. You like the pack. Can't run a pack if you don't have one."

"Tou-fuckin'-che, Jimmy. Always seeing through the bullshit has done you well old friend."

Ringo squeezed himself out of the cramped chair and sat on a rock close by the creek. Snoop bounded over to the big man, and Ringo scratched him behind the ears. "Yeah, that's it, little fellow. See, I'm not the big bad wolf you think I am." He turned his head to Jimmy. "But don't you go telling anybody I said that, or it's off with your fucking head."

"No problem here, Ringo." Jimmy laughed at the sight of Ringo playing with Snoop. Just one of Ringo's hands was almost as big as Snoop, but his gentleness around the small dog more than made up for his size when it came to the dog's acceptance of his attention.

"Anyway, what's on your mind there, Jimmy?"

Jimmy scratched his head, wondering where to start. But knowing Ringo, he didn't need to hear the whole long story. He just blurted it out. "I just found out I have a four-year-old daughter."

This turned Ringo's attention and his head towards Jimmy. It took him a moment to lift his large frame up from the rock, and he grunted as he leaned back up and wiped his hands on his pants.

"Well, holy shit, Jimmy! Congratulations! Sorry I ain't got a cigar or nothing for you."

"Don't worry about that, Ringo. I've got plenty to smoke."

"Yeah, bet you do. But a daughter? Holy shit, how the hell did that happen?"

Paraphrasing Crystal, Jimmy said, "Oh, you know, the usual way. Boy, girl, baby."

"Yeah, no shit, wisecrack. How did you find out? I know you don't carry a phone like the rest of the world. And you ain't got no post office box around here."

"She lives here. I met her in the park after the picnic yesterday."

"Ah, so that's why you're really here."

"No, not at all. It was a total surprise to me!"

"No shit, you have a daughter in Demry? Well, I'll be damned, Jimmy. You sly old devil you. Got your women spread around, do you?" Ringo laughed again, and he threw his big head back. "A sly old fox raiding the Demry hen house. Oh, that's too funny. I never pegged you for that kind of guy. But hey, a man's a man. And when in need!"

Jimmy let Ringo have his laugh and settle back down before he continued. "It's not like that at all, Ringo. She is a woman I know and spent a lot of time with."

Ringo lifted his eyebrows. "That woman you let mule with you for a while?"

"That very one."

Ringo leaned back against Jimmy's van and crossed his feet. He scratched at his brow and rubbed his hand over his bald head. "Damn, dude, a daughter. That's something else man. He rubbed at his face and brought his lips together in his fingers. "So, whatcha gonna do now?"

Jimmy rose up out of his chair and limped over towards the van. "I don't know yet, Ringo. I mean I been looking for this girl for a while, and then bam! There she is and a daughter to boot. Shit, this all just happened yesterday. Now I got this girl and this woman I want to see. I'm obligated to haul my load up to Colorado, but I feel funny just leaving like that. And, man, I just don't know what to do. I mean do I go to—?"

Ringo put out his hands and said, "Whoa, Jimmy, slow on down. Let's think about this for a minute."

Jimmy looked at Ringo as an unlikely ally in this situation. "Let's?" He pointed to Ringo and then to himself. "Like you and I?"

"Well, you asked me. So, yeah, like you and me."

"Sorry, man, I'm just confused." "First off, if you want to stay, I can help you unload or haul your stash. You trust me that far, don't you?"

"Of course. We've always been straight with each other in this arena."

"Okay, good. Damn, I always knew we would work together again! Now, about this woman and her daughter. Do you like this girl?"

Jimmy looked up at the sky and watched as the small clouds were congregating and racing across. "Ringo, I have never loved any woman the way I love her."

"And the little one? Did you meet her, too?"

Jimmy leaned back on the van and stood next to Ringo. His face was as close as it had ever been to Ringo's. He looked over at him and said, "She called me Daddy."

"Oh shit, dude! You're in now. Ain't nothing stronger than the first time you hear those words."

"Yeah, I had that feeling, too."

Jimmy and Ringo listened to the late afternoon breeze rustle the sycamore leaves. A wave of relief poured over Jimmy. He knew what he had to do. Ringo was right. He had never felt anything as strong as when Abby had called him Daddy.

"So, how the hell do I pull this one off?"

"Same way you pull off everything else, Jimmy. Be a man and do the right things. It's gotten you this far, hasn't it?

"So far I guess."

Ringo leaned back forward off the van and stood in front of Jimmy. "Tell you what I'm gonna do. I'm gonna take care of this load for you. Take me a few days, but I'll send someone up to help you out."

"Thank's. Just don't send that guy Steel. I don't trust him."

"Good call there; he is one mean son of a bitch. I got someone else in mind." Ringo laughed. "Matter of fact, he reminds me a little of you back in the day—young, hungry, and willing to play by our rules."

"Cool. I like that."

"That'll at least give you time to figure stuff out here for a while."

"I appreciate that, Ringo. I really do."

"Hey, no problem, Jimmy. Business is business. After that, I might have another proposition to run by you—something that can keep you in the money, but a little less dangerous."

"Oh yeah. What's that?"

"Let's just say the knowledge and skills you and I have acquired are pretty darn valuable out on the market. I been cooking something up for a while that might be right up our alley. But first things first. I'll fill you in when I get there."

"Cool, sounds intriguing."

"Could be, my man. You okay on cash for now?"

"Yeah, I'm good."

"Get a phone, Jimmy. Call me in three days."

"Damn, a phone! Never needed one of those before."

"Yeah, but you're a dad now. Welcome to the twenty-first century, old man!"

"Yeah, I guess you're right."

Ringo looked at the clouds that were beginning to form. "Well, partner, I better scoot before I get caught out here with you and your dog. Got to go see my own kids before they grow up and forget who I am."

"You're an easy guy to remember, Ringo. I wouldn't worry about someone forgetting you."

Ringo rubbed his head as he walked over to his motorcycle. "Guess you're right there, Jimmy."

Ringo straddled his large legs over his motorcycle and started it up. The Harley roared to life, startling Snoop, which sent him barking and running back and forth in front of the bike. The air filled with vibration that Jimmy could feel in his chest.

Jimmy held out his hand. Ringo wrapped his palm around Jimmy's and held it. Speaking up louder over the roar of the Harley, Ringo said, "You're doing the right thing, Jimmy. A lot of guys in the game would just cut and run. But I don't think you will, Jimmy. You're just way too cool for that!"

"Thanks, Ringo. You showed up just in time. I really needed someone to talk to."

"No sweat, Jimmy. That's what friends are for, right?"

Jimmy had a sudden awareness that despite knowing Ringo for years, he had never considered him a friend until just now. He gripped his hand tighter and said, "Nice to know I have some."

"Always, Jimmy. Fair to fun, brother. Make sure you call."

"You bet I will. And remember..."

"What's that?"

"Wheels side down! And thanks, Ringo James. Thanks for being my friend."

"No problem!" Ringo's smile flashed from beneath his beard. "Later on, Jimmy Star Two Fingers!" Ringo shook his head. "God, I just love saying that name."

Ringo revved up his trusty steed and rode down the road. Jimmy watched as he made the turn out of the campground and onto the pavement. He gunned it, and Jimmy listened to the powerful engine until it fell from earshot.

The quiet struck him quickly, and his thoughts turned to Crystal, Abby, and Claudette. He packed up his van and headed out towards town and the hospital.

Chapter 28

A n old tune Jimmy knew well accompanied him on his way back to town. He sang the final verse as it faded out, "Baby going on a feeling!" He let this verse repeat over and over in his head while keeping his eyes on the road. The late afternoon clouds were beginning to boil over their own banks, and the rain was beginning to coat the road in a soft puddle of grease, dust, twigs, and rain. The wheels of the van sprayed the rain from underneath its treads and made a hiss as they drove back up the canyon.

Jimmy's dinner with Crystal was soon approaching, but he felt the strong need to go to the hospital first and check and see how Claudette was doing. He knew that she would have plenty of friends and family to watch over visit and keep her company. He felt a kinship forming with her, and if he was to be in Demry for a while longer, he should act like it and make the most of his new friendship.

He passed the park where he met his daughter. A smile touched his heart. *That park changed my life. If I stay in Demry I am sure I'll be spending plenty of time there..*

He thought about all of the things he could do other than running dope up and down the state line, but none seemed that appealing to him. He was a pretty decent mechanic, and he thought that since there was waiting line at Gus's, it could be one possibility. The mine was another, but then he rubbed his knee and thought his age may be a detriment to getting hired to do such rugged work.

His years of running marijuana around the Southwest had paid him handsomely, and he had been smart about his money. So the thought of employment passed quickly. He would be fine on money for the foreseeable future. Ringo's offer of a future partnership was also something to consider, whatever it may turn out to be.

So many thoughts raced through his mind. What would happen tonight would certainly decide a lot. The old bugaboo of doubt snuck its way back into his head. Thoughts from the past—of heartache, betrayal, and loneliness—persevered in changing his gleeful mood to one of apprehension and mistrust of the way he felt.

What if she changed her mind? Or if she was just happy to see him after all of these years, but now the longing wore off? All of this flooded back into his heart as he pulled into the hospital parking lot.

"Snoop, you are gonna have to stay here, boy. Pretty sure pets are not allowed."

Jimmy cracked the front windows a bit. Closing the door, he said, "Guard the van, Snoop." He laughed every time he said this, knowing that while the bark was as sharp as his teeth, Snoop was no match for a serious invader.

Jimmy hobbled quickly across the parking lot, letting his sore leg drag, in fear of it buckling on the slick pavement. He turned back and retrieved his cane from the back of the van, and then slowly walked across the parking lot.

The starkness of the hospital entrance was a reminder that he was back in a place with rules and regulations. Something he learned in the Army and in his short stints in jail was that protocol was to be adhered to if you wanted to get where you were going. It wasn't much different than the unspoken and spoken rules that he and his other running partners had to remember to become successful in their own field.

The nurse at the front desk gave him the up and down with her eyes. "No umbrella, huh."

"No, sorry I left it back in Seattle!" Jimmy pushed his hair back out of his eyes and wiped his wet brow with the back of his hand.

The nurse peered up at him, and Jimmy gave her a big smile. She put her eyes back to the chart she was reading and asked how she could help him.

"I'm here to see Claudette Burns please."

"The nurse looked up again, this time smiling a little herself. "Boy oh boy, that woman has sure got a lot of friends. And here, all I knew about her is she is a tough old buzzard that didn't get along with most folks. Shows you what I know."

"She can be quite a handful when she wants to."

The nurse handed Jimmy a clipboard to sign. She took off her glasses and held them in her hand while looking at Jimmy. "You that man everybody in the park was talking about?"

"I surely hope not, ma'am. But I've noticed words and deeds around here travel with the speed of light!"

She stood up and peered over the counter while Jimmy signed his name. "Yep, you're him. They said he was carrying a cane."

"Who said he was carrying a cane?"

She took the clipboard from him and looked at the name. "Well, Mr. Star—oh, I like that name—half of this town seems to have some sort of story about you. Not uncommon around here, though."

"Well, I'm glad you like my name anyway."

"Third floor. Take a left when you get off of the elevator. Visiting hours are just starting, but the doctors have final say as to how long the patients can receive visitors."

"Thank you, ma'am. You've been very helpful, and, as far as the stories go, I hope they were more entertaining than the actual event. It was really nothing to write home about."

"So you say, Mr. Star, so you say."

Jimmy looked up at the clock behind the desk. It was five fifty-five. He had heard somewhere that seeing triple numbers on a clock was good luck, and your angels were looking out for you. "Excuse me, but do you have a telephone I can use?"

"Sure, there is a visitor lounge and cafeteria just around the corner. There is a courtesy phone in there."

Jimmy found his way to the cafeteria. A few people were scattered amongst the tables eating, reading, and sipping coffee. Jimmy fumbled through his wallet. His hands were shaking a bit as he looked at Crystal's phone number. He realized that there were only a few occasions when he had ever talked to her on a phone, and those were prearranged.

Jimmy tapped the number into the phone. He became anxious after the fourth ring, and she hadn't answered. On the seventh ring, an answering machine picked up, and he heard her voice. "Hi, this is Crystal. Leave me a message, and I'll fit you in somewhere. Bye."

He looked at the phone, disappointed that he wasn't speaking to her. "Uh. Hi, Crystal. This is Jimmy. I am at the hospital."

A short beep and Crystal picked up. "Jimmy, Jimmy—oh my god—are you all right?"

Her sweet voice flooded his memory and brought a smile to his face. "Oh, yeah, sorry, I'm okay. I'm just here visiting."

"Visiting? Funny place to be visiting."

"Oh no, I'm visiting a friend here. My friend, Claudette Burns, is in here for something. I'm not really sure what yet. I just got here.

"Oh, I heard about her today at the salon. I hope she is all right."

"Yeah, me too.

Jimmy watched a young mother with an infant in her arms negotiate a tray of food to a waiting table where two other children were sitting. He was amazed at her agility and with the ease that she had put food in front of the children and herself, all the while holding the infant.

"Jimmy, Jimmy, you there?"

"Yeah, I'm here, Crystal."

"Oh, Jimmy, I am so glad to hear your voice. I barely slept last night, making for a real long day at work today. With the funeral and all we had the family in early this morning. And then when the day got started for sure, I was just not at my best. I was so worried that I may have scared you off after introducing you to little Abby as her dad and all. I was so nervous I wouldn't see you again. I am going to see you again, aren't I?"

"Oh, you bet your'e gonna see me again. See me, touch me, feel me, and hopefully feed me. I'm getting hungry!"

"Oh, Jimmy, you're giving me a craving I ain't felt in some time."

Mmmmm! Jimmy stirred with excitement.

"Got some bad news for you, though."

"Bad news? What bad news?"

"Bad news is that I'm on my period. Our daughter sleeps in the same room as I do, and the roast I put in the oven for dinner, well, it's in the oven. I just never turned it on. So, it's gonna be a while before I can satisfy that need either!"

Jimmy laughed so hard his sides hurt. He had to hold the phone out away from his mouth in hopes of not breaking Crystal's eardrum. When he composed himself, he put the receiver back to his head. "Oh, Crystal, you crack me up, darling. God, how I've missed you."

"Oooh, Jimmy, I've missed you, too. I just want to be in your arms, baby. That's all I've ever wanted since I jumped out of the van. I was just trying to teach you a lesson that backfired on us. That's all."

The young mother caught Jimmy's attention. She was wiping down the table and gathering her children. He could hear her saying, "Okay, kids, let's go see Grandma now. But don't shout when you see her like you usually do. Grandma's tired today." The older of the children took the youngest one by the hand, and her mother by the other hand, and they walked out of the cafeteria. Her confidence and grace overshadowed her tired brow and urgent eyes.

"Crystal, I've got an idea."

"I'm sure you do, Jimmy. You've always been full of ideas."

"You got a car?"

"Yeah, I've got a car. Why?"

"Well, I'd like to see how Claudette is doing, and I thought maybe we could just meet and eat right here in the cafeteria at the hospital. I'm in here now. It smells pretty good, and it's nice and quiet in here."

"I'll be there in half an hour, Jimmy. Don't you go running off in the meantime with any of those pretty nurses."

"Promise! If I'm not in the cafeteria, I'll be on the third floor."

"I'll meet you in the cafeteria if you're still upstairs when I get there. People around here got enough to talk about without us adding any fuel for their fire. Not that I can give a hoot about what they think. I just want tonight to be about us. You, me, and Abby, all right?"

"Me too Crystal, see you soon."

Jimmy hung up the phone and leaned back against the wall. This was really happening. It was not an illusion. He would not be waking in his van from a frequent dream of Crystal. Someway and somehow, it had been seen fit for them to be together.

Jimmy brought a tray up to the third floor that had six cups of coffee, three teas, and a pile of cream and sugar. When he came around the corner to the waiting room, there were about a dozen people sitting, talking, and milling around. He didn't know if they were all there for Claudette, but the mood amongst them was somber.

Claudette's cousins, Ella and Rena, looked up and saw Jimmy as he came around the corner. Rena got up and took the tray from Jimmy. "Oh, Mr. Star, how nice of you to stop by!" Rena put the tray down and introduced him to the rest of the family members who were there.

"How is Claudette doing?"

"Well, she's got a nasty bump on her head. She's got a concussion, but she didn't have a heart attack, thank God"—Rena made the sign of the cross across her forehead and chest—"like we thought she might of."

"I heard she passed out, and that's why she fell."

"She did pass out, but we don't know why. It was hot out today, but not that hot. We're just waiting to hear on what some of the tests say. But for now, she seems to be doing all right."

"Well, that's good news, I guess."

"Good as any for now, Mr. Star, but boy, what a day. After this last weekend, the funeral, and now this. We are all pooped."

"I bet you are. Please have some coffee."

"Thank you. Please sit with us for a moment; we can't go in and see her right now. The doctors want her to rest, but she has been asking about you all day. She kept wanting to know if you had seen your little girl, and if you were getting married yet. We didn't know what she was talking about—if it was real, or just from the bump on her head. Do you have a daughter, Mr. Star?"

"Why, yes, yes. I do have a daughter." The confidence in his voice was much different than when Gus had asked him about children earlier today.

"Oh, that's nice," Rena said. "What's her name?"

"Her name is Abby."

"What a pretty name. I'm sure Claudette would like to meet her sometime."

"She just may get that opportunity, Rena."

"Well, you can wait here with us if you want to see her. I can't tell you how long it will be, but we aren't going anywhere."

"Actually, I am meeting my daughter and her mother downstairs in the cafeteria. But if I could visit anytime soon, I sure would like to. Claudette has been so kind to me."

"I'm sure she would like to see you, too. I'll come and get you if it's possible."

Chapter 29

Jimmy bought two more cups of coffee and sat down in the corner table near some wall length windows. Beyond the low hedges that lined the outside wall, Jimmy could see lightning over the far-off mountains. It silhouetted the sky and made the desert shine. Through the window, he could hear doves cooing and cardinals chirping as the Arizona sun was about to set.

He tapped his fingers across the Formica table. He was aware he was doing this, and although he was annoying himself, he could not stop. Finally, Crystal walked into the cafeteria holding Abby in one hand, and an umbrella in her other hand. Jimmy watched her tall body move gracefully across the floor. He admired the shawl she wore hung over her shoulder, exposing her smooth, tan skin.. As they came closer, he stood and waved. They both waved back. Abby wore a bright pink rain slicker, and matching boots.

Crystal fell into his open arms as they reached the table. She sobbed, and he could feel his neck getting moist. He held her around her shoulders and stroked her hair. "It's okay, baby. It's okay."

"I don't know why I am crying. I really am so happy right now."

Crystal leaned back and held him by the arms. She smiled, and he knew she meant everything she had said to him.

Jimmy felt a tug at his pants. Abby looked up at him with her big brown eyes and said, "Hey, what about me?"

Jimmy picked his daughter up and held her in his arms. She put her fingers in his beard and twirled the hair. She looked around along the floor and asked, "Where's Snoop?"

"He's out in the car, honey. We can't bring him in here."

"Well, can we go out and play out there?"

"We will, sweetie, we will."

Jimmy was stunned by what was happening. It felt like he had walked into someone else's life. But it was the life he had longed for and never thought he would have.

He didn't know what to say, so he asked, "You two hungry?"

After they ate, Crystal and Jimmy held hands as they recounted tales to Abby about how they met and the places they had been to. She was particularly interested in their stories of the beach. "Guess I might get that trip to California after all."

Crystal pulled a coloring book from her purse and handed it to Abby. Honey, me and your daddy have to talk for a while about some grown-up stuff. Why don't you color for a while?

"Okay, Mommy."

Jimmy and Crystal sat across from each other and held each other's hands. Their smiles were warming each other's faces. "Jimmy, look around, this is different than you're used to. There's walls and schedules and appointments and messes and compromises to make all the time. But this is my life now."

Jimmy looked around the room. A few families and nurses had made their way in and were quietly eating their dinner. "Not exactly the happiest of places for our first date again now, is it?"

"It's not about being in happy places, Jimmy. It's about being happy people. At least trying to be as much as is possible. I don't think that is something you ever gave yourself much of a chance for."

"I don't know if I would go that far."

"Maybe I'm wrong, and you have found that place of happiness I think we all long for. Well, at least I long for. Seems I know plenty of people that are just fine being miserable and all, but that's not for me. And I know it's not for you either, Jimmy."

Crystal reached over and stroked Abby on the back of her head. "Look, Mom, I drew a cat!"

"Hmmm, a green cat with a purple head."

"Yeah!"

Crystal looked back at Jimmy; he looked up from the drawing. They both smiled.

"I don't know what your life is supposed to be like, but this is my life now. And I don't know why I know this, but something deep inside of me tells me you are supposed to be a part of it."

"Maybe it is, because of this little girl right here. But I think you and I both know that the love we shared was honest, deep, and true. It's just that that lifestyle sucked after a while, and I couldn't take it anymore."

She looked around the room. "This is it, and this is where we live now. She's my heart, Jimmy, and so are you. I don't know how any of this can work out, and I would love for you to be a part of our lives."

Jimmy was tongue-tied. He knew that deep down, these things she spoke about his perception of happiness was long guarded and put away. He kept looking back to Abby drawing purple-headed cats and wondered if he could make this transition.

He had, for years now, always been afraid to dream and speak of what he wanted. But this weekend, being here in Demry and seeing how families worked and didn't work, all had changed his perceptions, and he knew that he would not be complete if he did not give himself this chance.

"Crystal, what you are saying is ringing so true for me. It's like you just reached in and showed me what I have been looking for all along. I just can't put the words together like you can. Too much pot maybe."

Crystal grinned. "Maybe, Jimmy."

"But I know I am at least willing to give this a chance. I owe it to you. I owe it to Abby, and I owe it to myself. Hell, what's the worst thing that can happen?"

"There is no worst thing with love, Jimmy. Just the lack of it."

"I know plenty about that, Crystal."

"Yes, I know you do, Jimmy. Lets make that go away. At least try to make it go away."

"I'd like nothing better, Crystal. This monkey has chased me every day since we've been apart. Not a day has gone by that I haven't thought about you and about what an ass I was."

"Me too, Jimmy. Me too."

Thunder rumbled in the distance. They looked out of the window and watched the display of light spread out over the horizon. The last rays of the sun crept out behind the storm, turning the mountains into gold.

"Beautiful out there, isn't it, Jimmy?

"Pretty beautiful in here also, Crystal."

Crystal turned her head and smiled. "I miss you, Jimmy. I really, really miss you. And sometimes, I miss the road. But that part I miss a lot less than you. Those mornings we would wake up and watch the sun rise over the desert when the crickets were still chirping, and the birds started singing, those were some of the best in my life. I wouldn't trade those days back for anything."

"I wouldn't either, Crystal. They are still out there, and I still get up before the sun on some days, but it's just not the same without you there."

Jimmy looked around the room again. "You know, I don't have any idea what life is like outside of the road. It's always been there."

"Jimmy, I'm not asking you to give up your life for me, for us. I just hope you'll stick around for a little while and get to know your daughter a little bit and spend some time with us. I know Demry may not be your kind of town. But who knows? You might like it here; you might not. I didn't think I would, but it grew on me after a while. Folks are nice here."

Jimmy looked at Crystal. His heart was pounding. He thought about all the miles he had put in over the last few decades. He was tired. He was bored. And he was lonely. During these last few days in Demry, he has had more real conversations with people than he has had in quite some time. And it felt good. It felt right to him in a way he couldn't quite grasp. He thought about what Nathan would say if he were here right now. He would probably be grinning and patting him on the back.

This was becoming very real, very quickly. The love and friendship he felt began to outweigh the fear of the future. Crystal stroked Abby's hair. Jimmy looked to the ceiling and silently asked, *Please don't let me wake up.*

Chapter 30

Rena walked into the cafeteria and looked around. Jimmy waved, and she came over to their table.

"Hi, Rena," Crystal said.

"Hi, Crystal. Hi, Abby."

"Hi, Rena." Abby said without lifting her eyes from her drawing.

Rena looked surprised. Her eyes got big. She put her hand to her mouth. "Oh my God, Jimmy, this is the little Abby? This is your daughter? Crystal, really?" She was shocked through her smile, but smiling nonetheless. "I-I-I mean how did you?"

"It's a long story, Rena," Crystal said.

"So, obviously, you two know each other."

"Sure do, Jimmy. Rena was one of the first women I met at the salon. Sit down, Rena, join us for a minute."

"Well, I'd love to, but I came down here to tell Mr. Star that Claudette has been asking about him, and she won't give no one there be until she gets to see him." Rena shook her head. "You know how she can be!"

"Yeah, I know, Rena. Jimmy, you better get up there before she comes down and gets you." Crystal smiled at

Jimmy and grabbed his hand. "Go ahead, honey. Me and Abby will wait down here for you."

Jimmy pressed the elevator button and waited for the door to open. His mind was racing as fast as his heart. In his life he had faced down the biggest bikers, the meanest cartel members, and the shadiest of drug dealers. But this was a challenge he felt ill-equipped for. This whole new world had been revolving around him the whole time he had been alive. He just didn't know it really existed. A world where people stay together, work together, and respect each other.

He gripped his fingers tightly in his fist. He became frightened at the possibility of blowing the whole thing. The door opened, and he got on the elevator. He watched the numbers light up and got out on the third floor. The visitors' area was a little quieter than before. Empty foam cups stained by coffee were sitting on the tray.

Claudette's cousin Ella told him that Claudette was waiting for him. Jimmy opened the door to her room. The bed she was lying in was inclined. There were tubes and needles taped to her arm. A large bandage covered part of her forehead. She looked a lot older than she did yesterday.

Jimmy walked over to her bed and stood by her. He put his hand on the railing. She reached up and touched his. He pulled away for just a second.

"Don't worry now, Jimmy. You won't break me."

"How are you feeling, darling?"

"Oh, I'll be honest with you. I have been better. But they say I will be alright." Her voice was low and crackled a little bit. "They got me on these pain medicines that are making me woozy."

"Yeah, Claudette, you are looking kind of woozy."

"I'm sorry you have to see me like this without my makeup and all. And my hair's a mess. Just got it done, too." She looked up at him and smiled. Her blue eyes sparkled through her pain. "I'm so glad you came to see me. "I've been worried about you all day."

"Worrying about me! Look at you, honey. You're the one we should be worrying about."

"Oh, Jimmy." She waved her arms around her body. "All of this stuff can be fixed up by doctors. It's all that other stuff they can't fix."

"What other stuff?"

"Matters of the heart, Jimmy. They haven't come up with the pill that can mend that."

Jimmy pursed his lips and shook his head in agreement.

"So, did you get to see her?"

"Yeah, I did."

"You ask her to marry you?"

"It's a little quick for that, don't you think? They are downstairs waiting for me."

"Oh, that makes me so happy. Are you gonna stick around for a while then?"

"I am, Claudette." Jimmy shook his head again. "I don't know what is going to happen, but I'm gonna give it a go."

"Don't you worry about all that figuring-out stuff. Your heart will tell you what to do. Just make sure you listen to it, or I'll have to come and chase you down."

Jimmy smiled and put his hand on top of hers. "Thank you, Claudette. These last three days have changed my life."

"Life's the same, Jimmy. It's your heart that's changed. You best be getting back to see your girls. I need to rest now. I'm just so sleepy."

Jimmy quietly left the room and got back on the elevator. When the door opened, Crystal and Abby were waiting on a bench.

"She gonna be all right?" Crystal asked.

"She's banged up, but she'll be all right."

"Are you gonna be all right?" she asked him.

He put her arms around her. "Yeah, baby, I'm gonna be all right."

He held her in his arms. She put her head on his shoulder and whispered in his ear, "I love you, Jimmy Star Two Fingers."

He felt a tug at his pants. He looked down at Abby with her little pink rain slicker on. Her big brown eyes were staring back at him. "Daddy, can we go get Snoop and go home now?"

"Yeah, sweetie, we can."

They all held hands and walked through the doorway. The storm had passed. The air was fresh and new.

The End

www.ingramcontent.com/pod-product-compliance
Lightning Source LLC
Chambersburg PA
CBHW030312200626
46816CB00002BA/865